Of Blood and Broken Light

A Risenfell Story

Aldric Thorn

The Steady Light Press

Copyright © 2026 The Steady Light Press
Curated by Aldric Thorn

All rights reserved.

No part of this publication may be reproduced, distributed, or transmitted in any form or by any means, including photocopying, recording, or other electronic or mechanical methods, without the prior written permission of the publisher, except as permitted by U.S. copyright law. For permission requests, contact The Steady Light Press.

The story, all names, characters, and incidents portrayed in this production are fictitious. No identification with actual persons (living or deceased), places, buildings, and products is intended or should be inferred.

ISBN 978-1-971917-01-6

Imprint

The Steady Light Press

The Steady Light Press publishes works of speculative and historical fiction concerned with memory, consequence, and endurance.

The volumes collected under the Risenfell record preserve accounts shaped by fracture, uncertainty, and survival, presented without imposed reconciliation.

Additional fragments, recovered materials, and ongoing records related to this volume are preserved at **risenfell.com**

Dedication

For those who carried the light, even when it burned.

Epigraph

Light does not fail all at once.

It thins.

It fractures.

And those who stand within it are changed long before they notice the dark.

   ~ Fragment recovered from an unmarked folio

Curator's Note

What follows is not a complete account.

The materials collected here; witness testimony, recovered folios, marginal annotations, and accounts preserved only through repetition were not created to agree with one another. In many cases, they cannot. Dates drift. Names shift. Locations refuse to remain fixed. This is not a failure of preservation, but a feature of the record itself.

I have not attempted to reconcile these fractures.

To do so would be to impose a coherence that the source material does not support, and perhaps never possessed. Instead, the fragments have been arranged with restraint, allowing the seams to remain visible where they insist on appearing. If the story feels incomplete, it is because it is.

Readers should understand that what is presented here reflects only what endured. Entire accounts are missing. Others survive only in contradiction. What remains was chosen not for clarity, but for consequence.

This collection concerns itself with one such consequence.

If meaning emerges, it will do so quietly, and at its own pace.

~ Aldric Thorn

Curator

ALDRIC THORN

(Filed under Fragment Set: BL–03)

Record of Preserved Accounts

Chapter One

The Last Daylight

By the time the sun slipped behind the treeline, Tavian Calder had already decided the light in Blackmere didn't set so much as retreat.

It went too quickly - one moment a thin wash of gold over the river and warped shingle roofs, the next a bleached gray that dulled edges and stretched shadows into long, grasping shapes. The villagers said it was the way of the valley, how the hills caught the sun and stole it early.

They said it the way men said things they did not believe but had learned not to argue with.

Tavian hefted the last crate off the skiff and set it down on the dock, boots thudding against damp planks. His shoulders burned with the day's labor, the ache deep and familiar. He welcomed it. Pain had weight. It kept his thoughts from drifting to places he'd spent years learning to avoid.

"Set that one by the post, Calder."

Jorren, the dockmaster, watched from beneath the shed's low eave, gray beard hooked in one calloused hand. Tavian obeyed, easing the crate into place.

"We'll sort it in the morning," Jorren added. "No sense tempting things this close to dusk."

Tavian glanced at the sky. The light was already thinning, draining from brass to pewter. It wasn't dusk yet. Not anywhere sensible.

"The river's calm," Tavian said. "Could run another load before it turns."

Jorren shook his head and spat into the water. "River'll be here tomorrow. Nightfall might not care for you if you're still working when it comes." He made a small sign over his chest, three fingers brushing bone. "You best be gone."

Nightfall.

The word had been circulating more in recent days, spoken softly, turned over with the same wary respect Tavian had heard men give to words like *siege* and *plague*. He'd heard it when he first arrived months ago, just another superstition in a forgotten town at the end of a bad road. But Blackmere's fear wasn't theatrical. It was practiced. Old.

"How close?" Tavian asked.

Jorren's eyes flicked east, toward the forest climbing the valley wall. "Tomorrow. Or the night after. Folk feel it in their sleep. Lantern oil burns wrong. Dogs won't settle." His gaze returned to Tavian, sharp and appraising. "You know the rules?"

"I've heard them." Tavian wiped his hands on his trousers. "Stay inside. Shut the doors."

"That's the half children get." Jorren leaned closer. "You don't speak the names of the dead. Not once the dark settles." A pause. "You lost anyone?"

Tavian's jaw tightened. He gave a small, practiced smile. "Everyone has."

Jorren studied him a moment longer, then stepped back. "Get your windows boarded. I'll see you come morning."

If morning came.

Tavian took his coat from its peg and left the docks. The river murmured behind him, steady and indifferent. It had been the one comfort he'd found in Blackmere, something that moved without noticing him.

The street sloped toward the town proper, a huddled sprawl of timber houses pressed together like men sharing a fire. Smoke curled from chimneys in thin, anxious lines. Doors closed as he passed. Shutters were drawn. The light continued to drain, and with it came a pressure behind his right eye - subtle, insistent, like a distant pulse he could not will away.

He did not look at the sky.

By the time he reached the square, most of the town had vanished indoors. Stalls stood empty, tarps lashed down tight. The well sat unattended. Only one place still bled light into the street.

The Latch.

Tavian hesitated, then pushed through the door.

Warmth and smell hit him at once, ale, smoke, damp wool. Familiar things. The tavern was dim, lit by a handful of oil lamps that cast more shadow than glow.

"Shut the door," the barkeep snapped. "You trying to invite it in?"

Tavian closed it quickly.

Mistress Halde stood behind the counter, broad-armed and hard-eyed, her hair braided tight. She relaxed a fraction when she saw him.

"Evening, Calder. Still hauling half the river onto dry land?"

"Someone has to," he said.

She slid a chipped mug toward him. "Same as usual?"

He nodded, set coins down.

"Nightfall's close," she said as she poured.

"So I'm told."

"If Jorren's saying it out loud, you listen." Her eyes lingered on him. "You shouldn't be alone when it comes."

"I manage fine on my own."

"Not the way Blackmere does things." She leaned closer. "You stay quiet. You don't answer knocks. And you don't trust familiar voices after dark."

Tavian lifted the mug, letting the heat seep into his fingers. "Understood."

He turned on the stool to scan the room.

A few locals hunched over their cups, voices low. Two young men studied a board between them, pieces carved from bone. In the far corner, chair tipped back against the wall, sat a man Tavian had hoped not to see.

Rovan Hollow.

Their eyes met.

The tavern fell away, replaced by a different silence, a different sky, one that had folded instead of darkened, spilling brilliance that burned without heat. Tavian's grip tightened on the mug until it creaked.

He looked away first.

"You know him?" Halde asked quietly.

"Lives near me," Tavian said. "Drinks."

"Mmm." She straightened. "Mind yourselves."

"Calder."

Rovan's voice crossed the room, flat and steady.

Tavian didn't turn.

Rovan was closer than he should have been when Tavian finally looked. Broader, heavier than memory, with gray threading his hair and a beard Tavian didn't recognize. A mug hung loose in his hand.

"You look almost honest," Rovan said.

"What do you want?" Tavian asked.

"To know how long you think you can outrun it."

Tavian's jaw clenched. "I came here to work."

"Sure you did." Rovan leaned in. "That why your eye shines when the lamps flicker?"

A muscle jumped in Tavian's face.

"Leave it," he said.

Rovan smiled without humor. "You think this place is coincidence?" His voice dropped. "The dark remembers you, Tavian. Always has."

A lamp above them guttered. For a heartbeat, the flame burned pale, bending toward the ceiling as if drawn.

Tavian's breath caught. Something cold stirred beneath his ribs.

Then the flame steadied.

The tavern breathed again.

Rovan stepped back. "Be ready," he said. "When the light breaks wrong, it comes looking."

He returned to his corner.

Tavian stood motionless, heart hammering.

Outside, the last of the daylight withdrew completely.

And Tavian had the sudden, unwelcome sense that Blackmere had been waiting for him far longer than he had been alive.

Chapter Two

The Warnings

Tavian did not remember leaving The Latch.

One moment he was standing at the counter, the pale flicker of the lamp still burning behind his eyes, and the next he was outside, boots on hard earth, breath fogging in air that had grown suddenly thin. The door was shut behind him. The tavern's warmth did not follow.

Blackmere had gone quiet.

Not asleep. Not empty. Quiet in the way a field goes still before a storm breaks, as if every living thing had learned the value of holding its breath.

Doors were closed. Shutters drawn. Smoke leaked from chimneys in narrow, anxious threads. Somewhere down the lane, a hammer struck wood, measured, urgent, refusing waste. Someone was boarding in for the Night.

Tavian stood in the square longer than he meant to, the silence pressing against his ears. The air tasted metallic, sharp enough to make his tongue prickle. He pulled his coat tighter and started toward the lane.

Halfway there, he noticed the markings.

They had been cut into the doors, high near the hinges, shallow but deliberate. Three vertical lines, then a diagonal stroke crossing them. Old work. Careful work. The kind done by people who expected to live long enough to regret mistakes.

He slowed, passing house after house. Every door bore the same sign.

When he reached his own, he traced the grooves with his thumb.

"Don't touch it."

The voice behind him was thin but certain.

Tavian turned.

The town elder stood a few paces back, wrapped in a shawl that looked as old as the houses themselves. Her hair was silvered close to the scalp, her posture slight, but her eyes were sharp, unblinking even in the dying light.

"Skin weakens it," she said. "Oil carries."

He lowered his hand. "What does it mean?"

"That you are accounted for." She nodded at the mark. "Not protected. Counted."

Tavian frowned. "Counted by what?"

She did not answer directly. Instead, she stepped closer and lifted his chin, angling his face toward the last of the daylight. Her fingers were cold.

Her breath caught.

She dropped her hand as if burned.

"Well," she murmured. "That explains why the valley feels... alert."

Tavian's stomach tightened. "What did you see?"

"Enough." She stepped back. "You have been touched. Not recently. Long enough ago that it's settled into you."

"I don't know what you're talking about."

"No," she agreed softly. "You wouldn't." Her gaze hardened. "Listen carefully. When the dark falls, you do not leave your house. You do not light flame. You do not speak your name. And you do not answer if someone calls to you."

"Even if I recognize the voice?"

"Especially then."

A cold ripple passed behind Tavian's right eye, subtle but unmistakable.

"And if I break a rule?" he asked.

Her mouth tightened. "Then it learns."

She turned away before he could ask more, vanishing down the lane with surprising speed.

Tavian stood there a long moment before unlocking his door.

Inside, the cabin smelled of pine and river damp. Sparse, clean. A cot. A table. A chair he'd mended himself. On the table lay a hammer and a stack of planks he'd brought home two days earlier, after hearing Nightfall spoken too many times in a single afternoon.

He lit a candle. The flame wavered, then caught.

He exhaled.

He told himself the town was feeding his nerves. That superstition had weight only when you gave it room. He had marched through valleys where men swore the earth itself would swallow you whole if you slept unarmed. None of it had been true.

He picked up the hammer.

One board per window. Measured. Placed. Nailed.

The rhythm steadied him. The sound was solid, real. The candle flickered at the edge of his vision, throwing shadows that twitched and leaned, but he did not look at them.

By the time he reached the last window, his hands were shaking.

He told himself it was fatigue.

That was when the scratching began.

Not loud. Not frantic. A slow drag along the outside wall, as if something were testing the grain of the wood.

Tavian froze.

The sound stopped.

He held his breath.

Three more strokes followed, lower this time, near the floorboards.

The instinct to explain it away rose immediately. An animal. A branch. The wind shifting.

Except there was no wind.

A pressure bloomed beneath his ribs, cold and insistent. Not pain. Awareness.

He stepped to the boarded window and pressed his ear to the wood. Nothing.

No breath. No movement. Just the absence of sound, complete and deliberate.

He stepped back.

"Not tonight," he whispered. "Not yet."

The scratching did not return.

He finished the last board and sank into the chair, elbows on his knees, hands clenched until the tremor passed.

A knock shattered the silence.

Three sharp raps. Firm. Confident.

Tavian's heart lurched.

Another knock followed, softer.

"Tavian."

The voice was unmistakable.

"Open up," it said. "It's me."

Rovan Hollow.

The elder's warning echoed in his mind.

Do not answer.

The candle flame leaned toward the door, stretching unnaturally thin.

Another knock.

"Tav. I know you're in there."

Tavian rose despite himself, taking one step toward the door.

Then he heard it.

Breathing.

Too slow. Too deep. Layered beneath the voice, like something learning the shape of it.

"Tavian," the voice said again... perfect, familiar, wrong. "Let me in."

He backed away.

The boards creaked softly as the pressure shifted outside, testing them. The candle guttered once, twice...and went out.

Darkness swallowed the room.

In the silence that followed, Tavian understood one thing with sudden, terrible clarity:

Whatever waited beyond the door had not come for Blackmere.

It had come for him.

Chapter Three

The Aftermath

T avian did not sleep.

The night dragged past in shallow increments, heartbeats counted, breaths measured, the dark pressed close enough to feel. He sat with his back to the far wall, knife in hand, eyes fixed on the door long after the breathing outside had faded into nothing.

Nothing did not mean gone.

When dawn finally came, it did not arrive all at once. The darkness thinned reluctantly, like a bruise refusing to fade. Pale light crept through the gaps between the boards on the windows, dull and colorless, as though the sun itself had second thoughts.

Tavian stood slowly, joints stiff, and listened.

Birdsong returned in cautious fragments. A door creaked open somewhere down the lane. Far off, someone coughed.

The world had resumed, but not cleanly.

He unbarred the door and stepped outside.

The lane looked unchanged at first glance. Frost clung to the grass. Smoke rose from chimneys. The same crooked houses leaned toward one another as they always had.

Then he saw the marks.

Deep gouges scored the wood beside his door... parallel grooves, torn fresh into the planks as if by something hard and patient. They were not scratches. They were measurements.

Tavian swallowed and looked up and down the lane.

Other doors bore similar scars. Some shallow. Some deep. One farther down had splintered entirely, boards hanging loose like broken teeth.

A woman stood there, staring at it. She did not cry. She did not move. She simply stared, hands hanging at her sides.

"Did you hear it?" Tavian asked quietly as he approached.

She turned to him with eyes too dry to be calm. "My husband opened the window," she said. "Just a crack. He thought... he thought it was our boy."

Her voice wavered, then steadied. "It wasn't."

Tavian had no words that would not make it worse.

She looked at him, then... really looked. Her gaze lingered on his face, his posture, the way he held himself like someone expecting impact.

"You," she said slowly. "It stopped outside your door."

Tavian's stomach clenched.

"How do you know?"

"I heard it move on," she said. "It lingered here longest. Like it was listening."

Other doors were opening now. Faces appeared, tight, drawn, searching. Murmurs spread through the lane like rot through timber.

Tavian turned away and headed toward the square.

The well was surrounded.

A small crowd had gathered,,, ten, maybe twelve people. More hovered at a distance, pretending to busy themselves while watching intently. At the center lay a bundle wrapped in a blanket, too small to be a man.

Tavian slowed.

Mistress Halde knelt beside the bundle, her broad shoulders hunched. The town elder stood nearby, hands folded, eyes closed.

"What happened?" Tavian asked.

Halde looked up. Her gaze sharpened when she saw him. "Boy from the river road," she said. "Went missing last night. Found him at dawn. Down by the old stones."

"Alive?" Tavian asked, though he already knew the answer.

"Yes," Halde said. "In the way a body can be."

She pulled back the blanket.

The boy's eyes were open, unblinking. His chest rose and fell. His mouth moved soundlessly, lips shaping words that never quite formed.

Tavian felt the pressure behind his eye surge, sharp and cold. He staggered a half-step back, catching himself on the well's stone lip.

The elder opened her eyes.

"It did not take him," she said. "It emptied him."

A man near the back of the crowd spat. "Never done that before."

"It has," another voice said. "Just not here."

The murmurs grew louder, turning on themselves.

Halde rose to her feet and fixed Tavian with a look that made something in his chest tighten. "You were here when it came," she said. "What did you see?"

Tavian hesitated.

Silence stretched.

"I heard it," he said finally. "At my door."

That set the crowd murmuring again, this time sharper.

"At his door?"

"Why him?"

The elder stepped forward. "Enough."

But the question had already taken root.

Rovan pushed through the crowd then, reeking of drink and sleep deprivation. His eyes went immediately to Tavian, sharp and assessing.

"You're still breathing," Rovan said. "Good."

"You came by last night," Tavian said.

Rovan nodded once. "I did."

"You knocked."

"I did."

Tavian's jaw tightened. "It used your voice."

That gave Rovan pause.

"Did it," he said softly. "Then it's learning faster than I hoped."

Several heads turned toward him.

"You know about this?" someone demanded.

Rovan ignored them. He stepped closer to Tavian, lowering his voice. "I left you alone after the tavern. Went back to my place. Didn't knock again." His gaze flicked to Tavian's door in the distance. "Whatever you heard wasn't me."

The pressure in Tavian's chest deepened, spreading like ice.

Halde crossed her arms. "Then why did it stop at your door, Calder?"

The crowd quieted.

Tavian felt their eyes on him... not curious now, but calculating.

He searched for a lie that would not make things worse.

Before he could find one, a shout rang out from the edge of the square.

"It's him."

Tavian turned.

A man pointed at him, finger trembling. "Ever since he came, things have gone wrong. The light. The air. The night..."

"That's nonsense," Halde snapped.

"Is it?" another voice said. "We've lived here all our lives. Never seen it do *that*."

The elder looked at Tavian again, and this time there was sorrow in her eyes. "You should not have come here," she said quietly.

Tavian felt the truth of it settle into his bones.

"I didn't bring this," he said. "But it knows me."

That was the wrong thing to say.

Rovan swore under his breath.

The elder raised a hand. "We will speak of this later. For now, the boy must be taken inside."

The crowd broke reluctantly, eyes still on Tavian as they moved away.

Rovan stayed.

"You feel it, don't you," he said. "Like a pull."

"Yes," Tavian said.

Rovan nodded. "Then it's closer than it's ever been."

Tavian stared at the pale sky overhead. It looked thinner than it had yesterday, stretched too tight.

"Why now?" he asked.

Rovan met his gaze. "Because you stopped running."

A tremor passed through Tavian... not fear, but recognition.

For the first time since he'd arrived in Blackmere, he understood something with brutal clarity:

The night had not come early.

It had come on time.

Chapter Four

Broken Rules

The first time Tavian realized Blackmere had begun dividing itself into *before* and *after*, it wasn't because of the gouges on doors or the boy's empty eyes.

It was because people stopped using his name.

He heard it in the way their voices slid around him like water around a rock. He saw it in how they turned their shoulders... not enough to look like fear, but enough to keep a line between themselves and whatever they suspected lived under his skin. Even Mistress Halde, who had never coddled anyone in her life, spoke to him like she was handling a knife by the blade.

Tavian returned to the docks out of habit. He needed the river to be real. The work to be simple. A rope hauled tight. A crate shifted. A plank underfoot that creaked the same way every day.

But Jorren met him at the edge of the wharf and didn't offer him a crate.

"You should go home," the old man said.

"I'm fine," Tavian replied.

Jorren's eyes stayed on Tavian's face a fraction longer than they should have. "Fine's not a thing we count on this week."

"I need work."

"You need quiet," Jorren said, and there was an edge in it now, something like resentment, as if Tavian's presence had forced the man to acknowledge fear he'd spent a lifetime managing. "You heard what the elder said. Stay in."

"I'm not a child," Tavian said, and the words came out sharper than he meant.

Jorren's mouth tightened. "No. You're not." He leaned forward slightly. "Which is why you should know better than to make the town stare at you."

Tavian clenched his jaw. "I didn't bring anything here."

Jorren made the same three-finger sign over his chest as he had the night before. "Maybe you did. Maybe you didn't. Either way, it seems to like where you stand. Go home."

Tavian turned away before he said something he couldn't take back.

The river sounded different today... still murmuring, still slapping its pilings, but like someone speaking in a room that had gone too quiet. Even the water seemed to mind its volume.

He walked the lane back toward the square.

Halfway there he saw Halde dragging a barrel across the tavern's threshold, bracing it against the inside of the door.

"Morning," he said.

She didn't look up. "It's not."

He stopped beside her. "The boy..."

Halde's hands paused on the barrel. For a heartbeat her expression softened into something like grief, then hardened again. "He spoke," she said quietly.

Tavian's stomach twisted. "Spoke what?"

She lifted the barrel's edge and set it, then finally faced him. "He said a phrase. Over and over. Not words I know. Not words anyone knows."

"And?"

"And when he said it," Halde murmured, "every lamp in the room leaned toward him like it wanted to listen."

Tavian felt the pressure behind his right eye tighten, as if in answer. Halde saw his flinch.

Her gaze sharpened. "You get that pain often?"

"It's nothing."

"That's a liar's answer." She wiped her palms on her apron. "The elder's coming tonight. She wants you at the tavern before last light."

"I'm not welcome," Tavian said.

Halde shrugged. "You're needed. Not the same thing."

Before he could respond, a shout came from down the road.

"Elder!"

People emerged from doorways like they'd been waiting behind them. A few stepped into the street, then stopped short as though there were an invisible line they didn't want to cross. Tavian followed their eyes.

The elder walked alone, moving with the same quick surety Tavian had seen the night before. She didn't look frail today. She looked like a person who had carried fear a long time and learned to use it as leverage.

She went straight to the square, and people gathered at a careful distance. Tavian held back near the edge, letting his presence be less obvious.

Rovan stood in the shadow of a porch post, arms folded, watching everything with the weary attention of a man who'd already seen the worst version of a day.

The elder lifted her voice. "No one leaves the valley," she said.

A murmur rose. Someone protested. "We have family…"

"You can mourn them later if you live," the elder snapped. The murmur died quickly.

She continued. "The rules hold. Doors barred. Flames banked. No names spoken after dark. No answering knocks." Her gaze swept the crowd, landing briefly on Tavian. "And no one goes to the old stones."

A man near the front shifted uneasily. "Why?"

"Because something there woke up." Her eyes narrowed. "And it does not like to be watched."

A woman's voice trembled. "Is this because of him?"

The woman's finger pointed before her courage caught up. Several heads turned, and Tavian felt the weight of their focus like a hand on the back of his neck.

Rovan moved first, stepping between Tavian and the crowd, as if that could stop their suspicion from finding its mark.

The elder held her gaze on Tavian. "It is because of all of you," she said. "Because you live here. Because you have lived here long enough to forget what it costs."

That did not satisfy them. It was too big, too abstract. Fear wanted something it could blame.

Tavian's voice surprised him when it came. "Last night it used a voice," he said.

The crowd quieted.

"It spoke to me through the door," he continued. "It sounded like someone I knew."

Several people flinched. One crossed herself and muttered something Tavian couldn't hear.

The elder's face did not change. "It copies," she said. "It tests. It learns the shape of a voice and wears it like a cloak."

Tavian swallowed. "Why would it stop at my door?"

A pause.

The elder's eyes sharpened. "Because you listened."

Tavian stared. "I didn't..."

"You did," she said flatly. "Even if you did not answer. You heard it. You leaned toward it. You gave it attention." Her gaze fixed on him. "That is how it finds the seam."

A seam.

The word landed wrong in Tavian's mind. It dragged at a memory he refused to unpack... the sky folding, light spilling through, men screaming without being touched. A *seam* in the world, opened and widened.

He felt sick.

The elder dismissed the crowd after that, barking orders, pushing people back to their houses. The lane emptied slowly, reluctantly, like people stepping away from a corpse while still needing to stare at it.

When most were gone, Rovan approached Tavian.

"You shouldn't talk in front of them," Rovan said.

"I'm done letting them invent stories," Tavian snapped.

Rovan laughed once, harsh and humorless. "They'll invent them anyway."

Tavian's hands curled into fists. "Then let them hear the truth."

Rovan's gaze held his. "You sure you want to say the word *truth* so close to something that likes listening?"

Tavian flinched at that... not because of superstition, but because he knew what it felt like to be heard by something that should not have ears.

He took a breath. "What do you know about Nightfall?"

Rovan's expression shifted, subtle, guarded. "Enough."

"That's what you said last night," Tavian muttered. "It's always *enough* with you. Enough to scare me. Enough to make me suspicious. Never enough to give me something solid."

Rovan leaned in, voice low. "Solid is how people die, Tav. They think they understand the ground and then it opens."

Tavian stared at him. "You followed me here."

Rovan didn't deny it. He didn't pretend it was coincidence.

"Yes," he said.

"Why?" Tavian demanded. "To watch me fall apart? To drink and sneer and remind me of what I left behind?"

Rovan's jaw tightened. "To see if it followed."

The words hit like a fist.

Tavian's throat went dry. "And?"

Rovan's eyes flicked toward the forest, then back. "It did."

A cold pressure bloomed beneath Tavian's ribs. The same awareness as last night, the same sensation of something waking and turning its attention, like a head lifting in the dark.

Tavian forced himself to speak. "What is it?"

Rovan's mouth twitched, not quite a smile. "If I had a clean name for it, I might sleep."

Tavian's anger cracked into something more raw. "Then tell me what you *do* have."

Rovan's gaze held, steady now, sober in its own way. "I have a memory," he said. "A thing I watched happen. A night the sky opened like someone tore it with both hands."

Tavian's breath caught.

Rovan continued, voice flattened by distance. "Light poured through. Not sunlight. Not fire. Brighter than it should've been and wrong, like it had edges." He swallowed. "The men closest to it screamed and fell. Not burned. Not cut. Just... emptied."

Tavian's knuckles went white.

Rovan's eyes narrowed. "And you..."

"Don't," Tavian warned.

"You stood up in it," Rovan said anyway, relentless. "Like you were listening. Like you heard something no one else did. And then you ran."

Tavian's pulse hammered. "I ran because the world was breaking."

Rovan nodded once. "Maybe." A pause. "Or maybe you ran because it touched you and you realized you were the seam."

Tavian felt the street tilt.

For a second he was back there... the split sky, the impossible brilliance, men dying without blood. Something cold inside him, like a hook placed deep. A sensation of being *noticed* by something that did not care how small he was.

He exhaled slowly, forcing his vision to steady.

Rovan watched him. "Feel that?" he asked.

Tavian didn't want to answer.

He did anyway. "Yes."

Rovan's gaze drifted to Tavian's chest, as if he could see beneath skin and bone. "It wakes when you get close to the truth," he said.

Tavian's voice went quiet. "You didn't tell me this before."

Rovan shrugged. "You didn't want it before. You wanted distance. Silence. A job. A river." His eyes hardened. "Now you have a boy in the square who can't blink, and a town looking at you like you're a door left open."

Tavian's stomach twisted. "What do we do?"

Rovan's answer was immediate. "We go to the old stones."

Tavian stared. "The elder said no one goes..."

Rovan cut him off. "The elder wants to survive. I want to understand what's hunting you."

"It's not hunting me," Tavian said, though he didn't know why he believed it.

Rovan's gaze sharpened. "Then what is it doing?"

Tavian opened his mouth.

No answer came.

Rovan's tone softened, only slightly. "We go before dusk. We look. We come back. Or we don't." His voice roughened. "But if we sit and wait, it'll keep trying doors until someone answers. And then Blackmere will learn what you already know."

Tavian swallowed, throat tight. "You're drunk."

Rovan's smile was a thin thing. "Not enough."

A bell rang suddenly from the far side of town, one sharp chime, then another. Not a church bell. A warning bell. A sound Tavian had heard in camps when scouts came in running.

Halde's voice carried down the lane. "Elder! Come now!"

Tavian and Rovan moved without thinking, bodies remembering old rhythms.

They reached the tavern to find a small crowd gathering, faces pale. Halde stood in the doorway, one hand braced against the frame.

"It's early," she said when she saw Tavian. Her voice shook. "The lamps are going wrong again."

Inside, the tavern's lamps burned, but the flames leaned, each one bending toward the back wall as though drawn by a current.

There was no wind.

The room smelled faintly of iron.

The elder stepped in behind Tavian and stared at the lamps for a long moment. Her expression hardened into something like resignation.

"It's beginning," she said.

Rovan's hand closed around Tavian's wrist, hard enough to hurt.

Tavian looked down at the grip, then up at Rovan's face.

Rovan was pale beneath the drink and grit.

"It's not waiting for Nightfall," Rovan said quietly. "Nightfall is coming to it."

Tavian felt the cold pressure behind his ribs deepen, as if something inside him had turned toward the sound of the bell.

And for the first time, he understood why the elder had warned him not to let it hear his name.

Because it already had.

Chapter Five

The Long Night

T hey went while there was still light enough to pretend the world had rules.

Halde tried to stop them at the threshold of The Latch, one broad arm braced against the doorframe like a gate.

"You go out there and you'll bring it back on your boots," she said. Her eyes flicked past Tavian to Rovan. "And you, Hollow, don't you look at me like this is bravery. This is stupidity."

Rovan's smile was a tired slash. "Bravery's for men who believe in clean endings."

Halde's jaw tightened. "And I suppose you don't."

"I believe in being alive tomorrow," Rovan said.

The elder appeared behind Halde, moving with that same sharp quiet. She looked at Tavian the way she had the night before, as if he were an equation she'd been solving her whole life.

"You were told not to go," she said.

Tavian held her gaze. "If we wait, people die."

Her eyes narrowed. "People will die either way."

"Not the same people," Tavian replied.

For a moment, something like respect flickered across her face, quick as a match struck in a storm. Then it was gone.

"You want to go?" she said. "Then take this."

She pressed something into Tavian's palm.

A strip of cloth, dark and stiff. It smelled faintly of old smoke and iron. Three diagonal cuts had been made in it, mirroring the marks on the doors.

"What is it?" Tavian asked.

"A reminder," she said. "That you are not cleverer than the dark."

Rovan snorted. "And if he is?"

The elder's voice went colder. "Then he will die faster."

She stepped back and let them pass.

Outside, the sky had the washed-out look of bone. The sun hung low already, though it was nowhere near evening. Light bled across the valley in thin layers, as if it couldn't commit.

Tavian and Rovan walked shoulder to shoulder, neither speaking much. Their footsteps sounded loud on the packed dirt road, too sharp for the stillness around them. No wind. No birds. Even the river's distant murmur seemed muted, like it didn't want to draw attention.

They passed the last of the houses and the fields gave way to scrub grass and thornbrush. Ahead, the forest rose dark and dense, an unbroken wall of trunks and shadow.

The old stones sat at the forest's edge.

Tavian had seen them once from a distance, a ring of half-buried slabs protruding from the earth like broken teeth. He'd assumed they were some old boundary marker, the kind of thing villages built and then forgot the reason for.

Up close, they felt like something else.

The stones were taller than a man, weathered smooth in places, cracked in others. Faint lines carved their faces, spirals, angles, marks that meant nothing to Tavian's eyes but made his skin tighten. Not symbols. Not writing.

More like scars.

Rovan stopped just outside the ring, breathing hard as if the walk had been longer than it was. He wiped a hand over his mouth, then stared at the stones like he expected them to speak.

"You feel that?" he asked.

Tavian nodded. The cold pressure behind his ribs had deepened since they left town. It wasn't pain. It was awareness. A tug... subtle, constant, like a hook threaded into muscle.

"It's like..." Tavian began, then stopped. He didn't have language for it.

Rovan gave a humorless laugh. "Like you're standing too close to a memory that isn't yours."

Tavian's throat went dry.

The air inside the stone ring looked wrong, thinner, almost shimmering. Not visible exactly, but *suggested* by the way the light distorted at the edges. Tavian's right eye burned faintly.

Rovan leaned toward him. "We don't go all the way in," he said. "We look. We listen. Then we leave."

Tavian stared at the ring. "And if it listens back?"

Rovan's mouth tightened. "Then we pray you're still the one it wants."

They stepped closer.

The ground inside the ring was bare earth, darker than the soil outside, as if it had been burned and never healed. No grass grew there. No roots pushed up. The absence felt deliberate.

Tavian's breath came shallow. His hand drifted to his ribs, pressing lightly, as if he could hold whatever stirred inside him in place.

He took one step into the ring.

The world shifted.

Not dramatically. Not with thunder or screaming light.

Just... subtly.

Sound dampened. Color dulled. The edges of the stones sharpened, as if the air between them and Tavian had been shaved thinner.

Rovan swore quietly behind him. "Tav..."

Tavian turned.

Rovan had not stepped in. He stood at the edge, boots just outside the blackened soil. His face was pale, eyes wide.

"You're..." Rovan whispered. "Gods."

"What?" Tavian demanded, voice sharper than he intended.

Rovan pointed... not at Tavian's face, but at his chest.

Tavian looked down.

For a moment, he saw nothing.

Then the light shifted, and he saw it.

Beneath his skin, under ribs and muscle, a faint pale glow, cold, bluish-white, like frost illuminated from within. Not bright. Not shining outward.

Just present.

Tavian's heart stumbled.

He staggered backward, and the glow dimmed slightly, but it did not disappear.

"That wasn't there before," Tavian said, though he knew it was a lie. It had been there. He'd just never seen it, never allowed himself to.

Rovan's voice shook with something Tavian hadn't heard in years. Fear.

"It's awake," Rovan said. "It's awake and it knows where it is."

A sound rose then, so faint Tavian almost thought it was his own blood moving.

A hum.

Not from the stones themselves, but from the air inside the ring. A vibration low enough to be felt more than heard.

Tavian swallowed hard. "We should go."

Rovan didn't answer.

His gaze was fixed on the center of the ring.

Tavian followed it.

At the ring's heart, the earth looked slightly sunken, as if something heavy had pressed into it long ago. A shallow depression. Blackened. Smooth.

And in that depression lay something Tavian hadn't noticed at first.

A strip of cloth.

Dark, stiff, old.

It lay folded neatly, as if placed with care.

Tavian's stomach clenched.

The elder's cloth burned in his pocket, suddenly heavy.

Rovan's voice was a whisper. "Don't touch it."

Tavian didn't move.

The hum deepened.

The air trembled.

And then, without warning, the light in the clearing *bent.*

Not dimmed. Not flickered.

Bent.

The sunlight above them warped, angling toward the ring like it was being pulled through a narrow opening. Shadows stretched toward the center, crawling over the earth like hands reaching for something lost.

Tavian felt the cold inside him spike.

His breath hitched.

The glow beneath his ribs brightened.

Rovan stumbled backward, nearly falling. "Tavian!" he shouted, voice cracking. "Get out!"

Tavian tried.

His legs wouldn't move.

It wasn't paralysis. It was *attention*.

As if the world itself had placed a hand on his shoulder and said, *Stay*.

The cloth in the center of the ring lifted slightly, edges fluttering though there was no wind.

Then a voice spoke.

Not aloud. Not in the air.

Inside Tavian's skull.

A whisper shaped like his own thoughts, but colder.

Return.

Tavian's vision tunneled. The clearing blurred at the edges.

He saw the battlefield again, the sky splitting, men screaming, light spilling through like something alive.

He saw himself standing at the center of it.

Not running.

Listening.

Rovan's shout sounded distant, underwater. "Tavian, move!"

The whisper inside him repeated.

Return.

Something shifted in the ring's center.

The depression in the earth deepened, as if the ground were softening. Darkness pooled there, not shadow, but something thicker, more complete.

A seam.

Tavian's throat tightened. He understood without understanding.

If that seam opened…

Blackmere would not survive it.

He forced his hand to move.

Clumsy, shaking, he pulled the strip of cloth from his pocket, the elder's cloth, marked with its cuts and flung it toward the center of the ring.

The cloth landed on the old one like a thrown gauntlet.

For a heartbeat, nothing happened.

Then the hum snapped into silence.

The bent light straightened like a released cord.

The glow beneath Tavian's ribs dimmed so fast it left him dizzy.

The darkness in the depression shuddered and collapsed inward, like something inhaling sharply.

Tavian fell to one knee, gasping, palm pressed to the earth.

Rovan rushed in then one foot inside the ring, then another grabbing Tavian's shoulder and hauling him backward. The moment Rovan's boots crossed the blackened soil, Tavian felt the world shift again, sound returning in a rush, color bleeding back into the trees.

Rovan dragged him out of the ring entirely and shoved him against a tree trunk.

Tavian's breath came in ragged bursts. His ribs ached as though something had tried to claw its way out.

Rovan gripped his collar. "What did you hear?" he demanded.

Tavian blinked at him, eyes unfocused. "It said..."

A distant bell rang from the direction of town.

One sharp chime.

Then another.

Then, without pause a third.

Rovan's face went white.

"That's the warning bell," he whispered. "That's not... that's not supposed to ring until dusk."

Tavian pushed himself upright, still shaking. "What does it mean?"

Rovan stared past him toward Blackmere, eyes wide with dread.

"It means," he said hoarsely, "the night is coming early."

Tavian looked toward the town.

Above the valley, the light had begun to thin again draining, retreating as if something had reached up and turned the day down.

And beneath Tavian's ribs, the cold glow stirred once more, faint, hungry, awake.

Top of Form

Chapter Six

What the Dark Knows

By the time Tavian and Rovan reached the edge of Blackmere, the bell had fallen silent.

That frightened Tavian more than if it had kept ringing.

The light was wrong again. Not night, still day, technically but thinned, washed out, like the world had been left too long in the sun and bled its color away. Shadows lay where they should not, stretching toward the town center as though drawn by gravity.

Rovan slowed, breath rough. "It's already ahead of us."

"Or waiting," Tavian said.

Rovan shot him a look. "Don't say that like you're inviting it."

They crossed into the first row of houses and immediately felt it, the pressure of attention. Curtains twitched. Shutters shifted. Someone barred a door from the inside with a sound like a coffin lid settling.

No one greeted them.

No one spoke Tavian's name.

They reached the square to find it half-cleared, as if the town itself had recoiled from the center. The well stood alone. The stones around it were bare. The boy from the river road was gone.

Mistress Halde stood in the doorway of The Latch, arms folded, face set into something like fury trying to pass as resolve. The elder was beside her, head tilted toward the sky as though listening for something no one else could hear.

"You broke the rule," Halde said as soon as she saw them.

Rovan opened his mouth. Tavian beat him to it.

"Yes."

The simplicity of the answer surprised them all.

The elder turned, eyes sharp. "You went to the stones."

"Yes."

"And?"

Tavian swallowed. The memory of the bent light, the whisper inside his skull, pressed close enough to make his vision blur.

"And something answered," he said.

A murmur rippled through the few townsfolk still brave enough to stand nearby.

Halde's jaw tightened. "You never go looking," she said. "That's how it learns the shape of you."

"It already knows me," Tavian replied, voice low. "Last night proved that."

Silence followed.

The elder studied him carefully now, no anger in her face, only calculation. "What did it say?"

Tavian hesitated.

Rovan shifted beside him. "Careful."

Tavian nodded once, then looked at the elder. "It wanted me to return."

A few people gasped. One man took a step back, crossing himself repeatedly.

"Return where?" Halde demanded.

Tavian shook his head. "It didn't say."

The elder closed her eyes briefly. "Then it doesn't need to."

She turned away, speaking to Halde in a voice too low for Tavian to hear. Halde's expression darkened further with each word.

Rovan leaned closer. "This is the part where they decide what to do with you."

Tavian's throat tightened. "And what do they usually decide?"

Rovan's mouth twisted. "Depends how scared they are."

A shout cut through the tension.

A man ran into the square from the western road, breath ragged, face flushed with panic. "It's back," he yelled. "At the far houses. The lamps..."

As if summoned by the words, the lamps along the street guttered.

Every flame leaned at once, bowing toward the same direction, the western edge of town. Glass lanterns rattled. Wicks burned pale.

The elder swore softly.

"That's not Nightfall," Halde said, voice tight. "That's..."

"Attention," the elder finished.

The man grabbed Tavian's sleeve, fingers digging in hard. "It stopped outside my door," he said, eyes wild. "Didn't knock. Just stood there." His grip tightened. "Then it moved on."

"To where?" Tavian asked.

The man pointed.

Directly at Tavian's house.

Something inside Tavian twisted, recognition sharp as a blade.

Rovan stepped between them again, shoving the man back. "Get inside. Now."

The man stumbled away without argument.

Halde turned on Tavian, fury burning through her restraint. "You led it back."

"No," Tavian said. "It followed."

"Same thing," someone hissed.

The elder raised her staff, striking it once against the stone. "Enough." The sound cracked through the square, sharp and commanding. "This is no longer a question of blame."

She fixed Tavian with a steady gaze. "You will not stay alone tonight."

"I don't need..."

"You will," she cut in, "if you want anyone else to live."

Tavian stiffened. "You're using me as bait."

"Yes," the elder said plainly. "Because it has already chosen you."

Rovan swore under his breath. "You don't get to make that call."

The elder's gaze did not waver. "I already have."

She turned to Tavian. "You will stay at the watchtower tonight. Alone if you must, accompanied if you insist. But you will be *seen*. That is the only way to keep it from testing every door in Blackmere."

Tavian's pulse hammered. "And if it comes for me there?"

"Then it does not come for the rest of us," Halde said, voice flat.

The words landed heavy and final.

Rovan looked at Tavian, eyes blazing. "You're not doing this."

Tavian exhaled slowly.

The cold pressure beneath his ribs pulsed once, answering something unseen.

"I am," he said.

Rovan grabbed his arm. "You don't know what it wants."

Tavian met his gaze. "Neither do you. But I know one thing."

"What?"

"It doesn't want the town," Tavian said. "It wants what's already inside me."

Silence fell again.

The elder inclined her head. "Then perhaps," she said quietly, "it is time you learned why."

A sound drifted through the square then... not a knock, not a voice.

A low hum.

The same vibration Tavian had felt among the stones.

The air itself seemed to lean toward him.

Rovan's grip tightened. "It's listening."

Tavian closed his eyes.

For the first time since the breach he barely remembered, he stopped resisting the sensation in his chest and allowed himself to feel it fully the cold, the pull, the awareness that something incomplete had noticed him again.

When he opened his eyes, the world felt thinner.

"I'll go to the tower," he said.

The elder nodded once. "At sunset."

Rovan shook his head. "I'm going with you."

The elder considered this, then looked back to Tavian. "You may bring one witness," she said. "No more."

Rovan released Tavian's arm only to clap a hand hard on his shoulder. "Lucky me."

Tavian didn't smile.

The light continued to drain from the sky.

And for the first time, Tavian understood that the darkness did not need to knock anymore.

It already knew where he would be waiting.

They did not leave immediately. Night needed to settle first.

Chapter Seven

The Town Turns

They heard the shouting before they saw the fires.

Not flames, no one dared that yet, but torchlight, banked low and wrapped tight, the glow muted and angry. It moved through the trees like a wounded animal, staggering and multiplying.

Rovan swore under his breath. "They didn't wait."

Tavian felt it before they reached the edge of the forest, the tightening in his chest, the way the light around the torches bent subtly toward him, like iron filings drawn to a lodestone.

Blackmere had gathered.

Men, women, old and young, faces drawn into hard shapes fear had carved quickly. Tools had become weapons in their hands, axes meant for wood, hooks meant for river nets, knives meant for meat. Someone had brought rope.

The elder stood near the well, staff planted firm against the stones. Mistress Halde was beside her, jaw clenched, torch held like a promise she did not want to keep.

The boy from the river road lay on a pallet nearby, watched by two women who flinched at every sound. His eyes tracked nothing. His mouth moved silently.

Tavian and Rovan stepped into the square.

The noise faltered, then surged.

"That's him."

"Don't let him get closer."

"He brought it here."

Rovan stepped in front of Tavian instinctively, hands open, palms out. "You want to talk," he said. "Then talk."

A man shoved forward. "We *did* talk. And then the night came early."

"The lamps," someone shouted. "They leaned for him!"

"That's not proof," Halde snapped. "That's fear."

"And fear keeps us alive," the man shot back. He pointed at Tavian. "You think it's coincidence that it comes to *his* door? That it uses *his* voice? That the stones wake when *he* steps near them?"

The murmurs swelled, feeding themselves.

Tavian felt the pressure inside him rise, not violently, almost eagerly. The sensation made him nauseous.

The elder struck her staff against the well. "Enough."

The sound cut through the square.

"We are not animals," she said. "We do not tear apart what frightens us and call it wisdom."

A woman near the back laughed sharply. "Then what do you call letting him stand there while the night listens?"

Tavian spoke before Rovan could stop him. "It's not listening to you."

Silence fell.

Several heads turned.

"It's listening to me," Tavian said for the first time feeling confident in speaking out.

Rovan hissed his name, but Tavian pressed on. "And if you send me away, it won't stop. It will follow."

The crowd shifted, uncertainty flickering.

The elder studied Tavian carefully. "You are certain."

"Yes."

"And if you stay?"

Tavian hesitated. The truth pressed close, sharp and cold.

"If I stay," he said slowly, "it will come faster."

The murmurs turned dangerous again.

"There," someone said. "He admits it."

"He's not denying it."

"He's daring it."

Halde took a step toward Tavian. Her voice was tight. "What exactly are you proposing?"

"That you stop pretending this is about blame," Tavian said. "It's about containment."

A man laughed harshly. "Listen to him. Talking like a scholar."

Rovan snapped then, his voice cracking like a whip. "You want to hear scholars? Then listen close."

The crowd quieted, startled.

"I was there," Rovan said. "When the sky tore. When men died without being touched. When something bright and wrong poured into the world and found him standing in the middle of it."

Several people crossed themselves.

Rovan pointed at Tavian. "You think he ran because he's a coward? He ran because he realized he was holding the door open."

The words rippled through the square.

Tavian's vision blurred briefly as the pressure beneath his ribs surged, reacting to the attention.

"He closed it," Rovan continued. "He closed it and lived with the cost while the rest of the world pretended nothing happened."

A woman near the well whispered, "Then why is it back?"

Rovan swallowed. "Because closing something broken doesn't mean it stays shut."

The elder's gaze sharpened. "And what do you suggest we do now?"

Rovan hesitated.

Tavian answered for him. "You give me to it."

The square exploded.

"No!"

"That's madness."

"You'll doom us all."

Rovan spun on him. "You don't get to decide that."

"I already did," Tavian said quietly.

The elder raised her hand again, commanding silence with the weight of authority earned over years. "Explain."

Tavian took a breath. The air felt thin enough to tear.

"It isn't here for the town," he said. "It's here because of what it couldn't finish. If I remove myself... if I go where it expects me to be, it will follow. And it will stop testing your doors."

A man sneered. "You expect us to believe it won't just come back?"

"I expect you to believe I'm the seam it keeps pressing against," Tavian said.

The elder's eyes flicked to his chest, then back to his face. "You are certain."

"Yes."

Silence stretched.

Then Halde spoke, voice low. "Where would you go?"

Tavian looked toward the watchtower rising above the western ridge.

Rovan swore softly.

The elder closed her eyes for a long moment. When she opened them, they were steady.

"Tonight," she said. "Before full dark. You will go to the tower."

Rovan stepped forward. "He won't be alone."

The elder studied him. "You would bind yourself to this?"

Rovan met her gaze. "I already am."

She nodded once. "Then you will both go."

The crowd murmured, but something had shifted. Fear had found a shape it could act on.

The elder raised her staff. "We do not kill him," she said. "We do not exile him. We do not pretend he is nothing." Her gaze swept the crowd. "We acknowledge what has come to us, and we do not meet it with chaos."

A man shouted, "And if he lies?"

Tavian met the man's eyes. "Then you won't have to worry about me ever coming back."

That quieted them.

The elder turned to Tavian. "You will go at sunset. You will not flee. And you will not invite it."

Tavian nodded.

Rovan's hand closed around his forearm, hard. "You don't get to do this alone."

Tavian looked at him. "I'm not."

Above them, the sky dimmed another shade, as if the day itself were folding inward.

The torches leaned again.

Someone screamed.

At the edge of the square, the boy on the pallet jerked violently, his body arching. His mouth opened wide, and this time a sound came out... a single, broken syllable that scraped the inside of Tavian's skull.

He staggered, vision swimming.

Rovan caught him.

The elder stared at the boy, then at Tavian.

"It knows you're ready," she said.

Tavian forced himself upright.

"No," he said softly. "It knows I've stopped pretending."

The light drained further, shadows stretching long and eager across the stones.

And Blackmere, having chosen its answer, stepped back and let the night finish approaching.

Chapter Eight

The Breach Remembered

The town did not follow them when they left the square.

That was the mercy.

They moved through Blackmere without hurry, without ceremony. Torches were already being banked behind shutters. Doors closed softly as they passed. Not slammed. Not barred in panic. Closed with the careful finality of people who had decided where the danger belonged.

Behind them, the square emptied.

Ahead, Tavian's house waited... dark, narrow, ordinary.

Rovan did not speak until they were inside and the door was shut.

Tavian slid the bar home and leaned his weight against it for a moment longer than necessary. His breath came shallow, not from fear, but from the pressure still clinging to him, the sense of being watched by something patient enough to wait.

Rovan crossed the room and lit a single lamp. The flame wavered, leaned slightly, then steadied.

Both men noticed.

Neither commented.

Tavian exhaled and pushed away from the door. The room smelled of pine and old river damp. Familiar. Real. A place that had weight. He went to the table and sat, elbows braced, hands clasped tightly enough that his knuckles whitened.

Rovan remained standing.

"You shouldn't have said it like that," Rovan said finally. Not accusation. Observation.

"I know," Tavian replied.

"But you meant it."

"Yes."

Rovan nodded once. He dragged a chair back with his boot and sat opposite Tavian, forearms resting on his thighs, posture loose in a way that suggested he was trying very hard not to crowd him.

Silence settled.

Outside, the town breathed carefully.

"You keep remembering it wrong," Rovan said.

Tavian's jaw tightened. "I know."

"No," Rovan said gently. "You know now. You didn't before."

Tavian stared at the tabletop. The wood grain swam slightly at the edges of his vision. "I told myself the version I could live with."

Rovan leaned back. "We all do."

The lamp hissed softly.

Tavian swallowed. "You said I stood."

"Yes."

"In the light."

"Yes."

"And then I ran."

Rovan shook his head. "And then you left."

The distinction landed harder than Tavian expected.

"I don't remember choosing," Tavian said quietly.

"That's because you weren't choosing between courage and fear," Rovan replied. "You were choosing between dying there and dying later."

Tavian closed his eyes.

The memory rose... not like a dream, not like a vision. Like a wound being pressed.

The battlefield came back whole.

Not chaos.

Quiet.

Too quiet.

Men lay where they had fallen, some twisted, some unnaturally still, their faces caught in expressions that did not belong to sleep or death. The sky above them had folded instead of darkened, a seam creased through it like fabric pulled too tight.

Light poured through that seam.

Not fire. Not lightning.

Heavy. Silent.

Wrong.

Tavian felt it again, the pressure against his chest, the impossible sense of something *aware* noticing him noticing it.

He had stepped forward.

Not because he was brave.

Because he had believed terribly, rationally that understanding it might stop it.

"I heard it," Tavian said, voice barely above a whisper. "Not with my ears. With... recognition."

Rovan didn't interrupt.

"It wasn't calling for help," Tavian continued. "It was... incomplete. Like something half-open, half-falling."

He swallowed. "I thought if I listened, if I stayed still long enough, I could figure out how to close it."

The light had pulsed.

The seam had widened.

Men had screamed.

And something inside him had torn loose.

Not outward.

Away.

Tavian pressed his palm flat against his sternum, grounding himself in the present. "When I finally pulled back, it wasn't because I was afraid of it."

Rovan's voice was steady. "It was because you realized what it was doing to you."

"Yes." Tavian's throat tightened. "And what it would keep doing if I stayed."

Silence stretched.

Then Rovan said it.

"I don't blame you."

Tavian looked up sharply.

Rovan met his gaze without flinching. "I blamed you for years," he said. "That's not the same thing."

Tavian's breath hitched. "Rovan..."

"Listen," Rovan cut in, not harshly. "I watched the sky tear open. I watched men die without being touched. I watched you stand there longer than anyone else could have."

His voice roughened. "And when you left, I told myself you'd run. Because if you'd stayed... none of us would've walked away."

Tavian's hands shook. "I left them."

Rovan shook his head. "You left *me*," he said. "And that's the part I had to forgive."

The words settled between them, heavy and honest.

Rovan leaned forward, forearms on his knees. "If I'd been the one standing there, if it had been listening to *me*..." He exhaled sharply. "I would've done the same damn thing."

Tavian's chest tightened painfully.

"You didn't abandon us," Rovan said. "You broke something you didn't understand and survived long enough to carry it."

Tavian stared at him. "You don't know that."

Rovan's mouth twitched into something like a sad smile. "I know you. That's enough."

The lamp flickered again, just once.

Tavian felt the cold pressure beneath his ribs stir faintly, like a scar responding to weather.

Rovan noticed.

"You feel it now," he said.

"Yes."

"And you felt it then."

Tavian nodded. "That's why it followed."

Rovan exhaled slowly. "And that's why we're going to the tower."

Tavian looked toward the door, toward the darkened town beyond it. Blackmere lay quiet now, not safe, not yet, but decided.

"We'll leave at first light," Tavian said.

Rovan nodded. "We'll be gone before fear changes its mind."

They sat in silence after that... not empty silence, but shared.

Two men holding the same memory from opposite ends.

Outside, night finished settling over Blackmere. Shadows stretched. Lamps burned low but steady. The town, having chosen its answer, did not look back.

Inside the house, Tavian Calder finally allowed himself to remember the breach as it had been.

Not as cowardice.

Not as failure.

But as the moment something unfinished chose him, and he survived long enough to finish it.

Chapter Nine

Faultlight

They left Blackmere before the sun surrendered fully; the town already looked like it was bracing for loss.

No one followed them.

Not truly.

A few shapes hovered behind shutters. A few faces drifted in and out of window-light like uneasy spirits. Rope had been brought out and taken back in again. The square carried the faint smell of smoke from banked lamps, as if the town had decided even fire should lower its voice.

Tavian walked with his hands loose at his sides, forcing his posture into something that resembled calm. It was a soldier's trick: move like you aren't afraid and you can sometimes convince your body to stop shaking.

It didn't work.

The valley felt tighter than it had yesterday. Not in the air, not in the weather. Tight like a drawn bowstring. He could feel attention in the space around him, a pressure that thickened when he passed certain doorways, eased when he stepped beyond them, then returned again as if remembering.

The world, it seemed, had learned he existed.

Rovan stayed half a pace behind him, close enough that Tavian could sense his body heat, close enough that if Tavian stumbled, he'd hit Rovan before the ground.

"You sure you want to walk out like this?" Rovan muttered.

Tavian didn't look back. "Like what?"

"Like you're already dead," Rovan said.

Tavian felt his mouth tighten. "If I look alive, they'll try to keep me."

Rovan gave a sound that might have been a laugh if it hadn't been shaped like pain. "They don't know how to keep anything."

They reached the square.

Mistress Halde stood in The Latch's doorway, arms folded, torch lowered, face set into the kind of hardness that came from surviving too many nights by refusing to soften. She watched Tavian without speaking, but her eyes said what her mouth wouldn't:

If you fail, you take us with you.

The elder waited near the road. Alone. Staff planted firm in earth that had been trod by generations who'd learned where not to linger.

She looked at Tavian the way she had the night before... like he was not merely a man, but a condition the valley had been holding back for a long time.

"You will not be watched," she said.

Rovan's jaw tightened. "He's being watched right now."

The elder's gaze flicked to him. "By fear," she replied. "Not by help."

Tavian stepped closer. The elder's eyes moved over him, not reading his face but the spaces around him, like she could see currents in air that Tavian could only feel.

"The lamps leaned again," she said quietly.

Tavian nodded once.

"And you went to the stones," she continued, voice steady. "And something answered."

Tavian didn't deny it.

The elder reached into her shawl and produced a folded strip of cloth. This one was older than the one she'd given him before... stiffer, darker, as if soaked long ago and dried in smoke. Three shallow cuts crossed its surface, not decorative, not symbolic in any comforting way. The marks looked like scars somebody had decided to preserve.

"Take this," she said.

Tavian hesitated. The cloth seemed heavier than it should have been. Not by weight, by *history*.

"What is it?" he asked.

The elder's mouth tightened. "A boundary."

Rovan snorted. "Cloth doesn't make boundaries."

"No," the elder agreed, "but memory does."

The first had been a warning. This was a remembrance.

Tavian took it. The fabric was cold despite being in her hand. It smelled faintly of iron and old ash, and when his fingers closed around it, he felt a small, sharp tightening beneath his ribs, as if something inside him had noticed.

He didn't like that.

He tucked the cloth into his coat without looking at it again.

The elder watched him do it. "Good," she murmured.

Rovan shifted, restless. "If you're going to say what you think, say it."

The elder's gaze returned to Tavian. "You want to know what it is you carry."

Tavian's throat tightened. He wanted to deny it... to insist he was just a man, just a deserter, just a laborer. But the night had already proven that lie thin.

"Yes," he said.

The elder studied him a long moment. Then she glanced around the square, the closed doors, the drawn shutters, the careful distance people kept even from their own neighbors.

"Names are dangerous," she said.

Rovan's voice sharpened. "Then don't say it."

"I have not said it in years," the elder replied. "Not aloud. Not where a threshold could hear." Her gaze flicked to Tavian's chest, then to his eyes. "But you are going to stand on a tower with nothing between you and the valley's listening."

Tavian felt the cold pressure behind his right eye tighten as if in agreement.

The elder stepped closer until Tavian could smell the herbs in her shawl, both bitter and sharp, the scent of things meant to ward off rot.

"When I speak it," she said, voice dropping, "you do not repeat it."

Tavian nodded once.

Rovan leaned in, suddenly still. Even he seemed to understand instinctively that something ceremonial was happening.

The elder took a breath and spoke the word like a blade being drawn.

"Faultlight."

It did not sound like a spell.

It sounded like a diagnosis.

The syllables landed inside Tavian's skull with a weight that made his teeth ache.

The world around them seemed to pause. Not in time, just in attention. A subtle tightening, as if the valley itself had leaned closer to hear the word and then decided it didn't like what it meant.

Tavian's breath left him slowly.

Rovan whispered, "That's what this is?"

The elder nodded, once. "Light that broke and did not mend," she said. "Light that learned the shape of damage." Her eyes sharpened. "Light that remembers being torn."

Tavian swallowed. The name made his condition feel older than him. It made his ribs feel less like a wound and more like a hinge in a door the world had never properly closed.

Rovan stared at Tavian, then back to the elder. "You're saying it's... what? A sickness?"

"No," the elder said, almost impatient. "A consequence."

Tavian's mouth went dry. "Of what?"

The elder's gaze drifted past Tavian toward the forest and the dark silhouette of the watchtower on the ridge.

"Of a seam in the sky," she said. "Of a wrongness that crossed. Of a moment when the world folded and a portion of illumination behaved like a wound."

Tavian felt the memory stir, sharp and hot behind the cold.

The elder continued, voice flat with long familiarity. "Blackmere marks its doors because once, long ago, the valley learned that thresholds matter when the light breaks wrong. Not to keep it out." Her eyes narrowed. "To tell it which homes have already been counted."

Tavian's stomach dropped.

He thought of the gouges on doors.

Thought of the way the thing had paused outside his threshold, breathing slow beneath a stolen voice.

Rovan asked the question Tavian couldn't. "How do you know all this?"

The elder's face did not soften. "Because I was taught. Because my mother was taught. Because my mother's mother watched a night when the valley's stars vanished and the lamps bent toward a single door like they were praying to be extinguished."

Tavian felt his pulse quicken.

"And because," the elder added quietly, "I have seen it in men who come home from wars that should not exist."

Rovan's jaw tightened.

Tavian's ribs tightened.

The elder stepped closer and touched Tavian's sternum with two fingers... firm, like testing the bruise beneath skin.

Tavian flinched.

Something inside him responded.

Not outwardly visible, but in sensation: a cold pulse, a pressure shifting, as if the thing beneath his ribs had turned toward her touch.

The elder withdrew her hand at once.

"There," she whispered. "It answers being noticed."

Rovan's face went hard with anger. "Don't touch him."

"He needs to understand he is not merely haunted," the elder replied. "He is aligned."

Tavian stared. "Aligned with what?"

The elder's eyes narrowed as if she weighed whether to answer. At last she said, "With what tried to cross."

Rovan made a sharp sound. "So it *is* hunting him."

The elder shook her head. "Hunting implies hunger." Her gaze returned to Tavian. "This is not hunger."

Tavian's voice was thin. "Then what is it?"

The elder's lips pressed together. When she spoke, the words were careful, and that care scared Tavian more than blunt fear.

"It is an unfinished crossing," she said. "A passage that did not complete. A door that did not close clean." Her gaze hardened. "And faultlight is the residue of that failure, the cold brightness left behind when the world tore and tried to stitch itself shut around you."

Tavian's breath caught. The phrase *around you* felt like a hand closing.

Rovan stared at Tavian's chest, as if he expected to see something glowing through skin. "And it can... speak through it."

"Yes," the elder said. "Because it is a bridge. A fracture that still connects."

Tavian's throat tightened. He remembered the whisper at the stones.

Return.

He remembered the sensation of attention in the dark.

Rovan's voice dropped. "What does it want?"

The elder did not answer immediately. She looked past Tavian toward the watchtower again, toward the thinning light, toward the place the night seemed to be gathering too early.

Then she said, quietly, "It wants the break to stop hurting."

Tavian blinked. The words felt wrong. Human.

The elder's gaze sharpened. "Not because it is merciful," she added. "Because a break that remains open threatens everything around it." Her eyes held Tavian's. "It wants the world to mend where it was torn."

"And what does it cost?" Tavian asked, voice rough.

The elder's expression tightened into something like grief tempered by practicality. "Whatever is easiest to cut away."

Silence fell.

In the distance, the warning bell sounded once... low, long, not a call so much as a confession the town could no longer deny.

The light over the valley thinned further, draining toward gray. Not sunset. Not weather. A tightening. A deliberate retreat.

Tavian felt the cold brightness beneath his ribs pulse in answer, almost eager now that it had been named.

He hated that.

Halde's voice drifted from the tavern doorway, rough and low. "Go."

Tavian turned and met her eyes. She did not offer encouragement. She did not offer prayer.

She offered permission to leave before fear turned back into violence.

Rovan's hand found Tavian's sleeve, gripping hard. "We go now," he said. "Before they decide they'd rather hang you than wait."

The elder lifted her staff slightly. "Listen," she said to Tavian as he started to turn away.

Tavian paused.

"If it speaks in your head," the elder murmured, "do not answer with words." Her eyes held his. "Answer with refusal. With certainty. With your own will." A pause. "It cannot take what you do not offer."

Tavian nodded once.

They started toward the ridge.

The road out of town felt narrower than before, as if the valley itself had drawn in. The trees stood too still. The air tasted of iron again.

Halfway up the slope, Tavian's vision flickered, not blacking out, not blurring, but shifting just enough that he felt the world's edges soften. The cold brightness beneath his ribs pulsed, and this time it felt like a hand pressing outward.

Rovan noticed Tavian's stumble. "Tav."

Tavian swallowed. "I'm fine."

Rovan's eyes narrowed. "Don't lie to me."

Tavian exhaled slowly. "I can feel it," he admitted.

Rovan went still. "Feel what?"

Tavian stared at the watchtower's silhouette ahead. It looked less like a lookout now and more like a needle pushed through the valley's skin.

"It knows we're coming," Tavian whispered.

The hum in the air deepened as if in answer.

Not loud.

Not dramatic.

Just present, like an instrument being tuned before a performance.

Rovan's hand slid down to the knife at his belt. He didn't draw it. He knew steel would mean nothing. But the gesture was human, and humans needed gestures when stepping into the unknown.

The light drained another degree.

Tavian felt the cold brightness inside him pulse again, small, insistent, like a heartbeat that was not quite his.

And as the tower loomed closer, Tavian understood something with sudden, terrible clarity:

Nightfall was not arriving early out of impatience.

It was arriving because something in the valley had begun to pull the night down by the throat.

Chapter Ten

The Listening Dark

They did not speak as they left the square.

Not because they had agreed not to, but because the silence had begun to feel... attentive. As if words were objects now, heavy things that could be set down and examined by whatever moved just beyond the reach of sight.

Tavian felt it most clearly when he tried to breathe too deeply. The air resisted him, not with pressure, not with pain, but with a strange, patient reluctance, like a door that would open eventually if pushed long enough.

Rovan noticed it too.

"You feel that," Rovan murmured, finally. He kept his voice low, pitched carefully between breaths. "Like the world's got an ear pressed to us."

Tavian nodded once.

They took the western road again, but the path had lost its sense of direction. It was still dirt and stone beneath their boots, still hemmed in by brush and low trees, but the distance between steps felt inconsistent. Sometimes Tavian would take three strides and feel like he'd barely moved. Other times a single step would carry him farther than it should.

The moon rose higher, thin and pale, casting a weak, uneven light that seemed to slide off the ground rather than settle on it.

"Don't like this," Rovan said. "Night's supposed to *arrive*. This one's... spreading."

Tavian's ribs tightened with a familiar cold awareness.

"It's not night," Tavian said. "Not yet."

Rovan shot him a look. "You sure about that?"

Tavian slowed, scanning the treeline. The forest stood unnaturally still. No wind moved the branches. No insects sang. Even the faint rustle of small animals... always present if you listened for it, was gone.

The dark between the trees looked thicker than it should have been, pooling in hollows, stretching in elongated fingers toward the road.

"I'm sure," Tavian said. "This is something else wearing its shape."

They walked on.

The first voice came from behind them.

"Tavian."

It was soft. Casual. Almost bored.

Rovan spun, knife half-drawn.

The road behind them was empty.

No movement. No sound.

Tavian felt the pressure behind his eye spike, sharp and cold.

"Don't," Rovan hissed. "Don't answer."

Tavian didn't speak. He stared at the empty road, jaw clenched.

The voice came again, closer this time, though there was no one there.

"You don't have to keep walking," it said. "You're tired."

Rovan took a step closer to Tavian, shoulder brushing his. "It's not me," he said quickly. "You hear that, right? It's not me."

"I know," Tavian said.

The voice shifted then... subtly, precisely.

"Tav."

Rovan went rigid.

Tavian's chest tightened painfully. He swallowed hard, forcing himself to breathe shallowly.

The voice had Rovan's cadence now. Not perfect, too smooth around the edges, but close enough to make Tavian's muscles react before his mind could stop them.

"Don't turn," Rovan whispered. "I didn't say it."

"I know," Tavian repeated, though the word felt thinner the second time.

The dark between the trees stirred, not with motion but with *attention*. Tavian had the sudden, uncomfortable impression that the forest was leaning closer, like an audience drawing in toward a stage.

The voice sighed. "You always were stubborn."

Tavian squeezed his eyes shut.

The elder's words returned unbidden: *Do not answer with words. Answer with refusal. With certainty.*

He pictured the cold brightness beneath his ribs, not as a threat, not as a promise, but as something *contained*. A pressure he could brace against.

He kept walking.

The voice followed them.

It tried other tones. Other shapes.

A woman's whisper, trembling with fear.A child's confused question.A familiar laugh from a long-dead comrade Tavian had not thought of in years.

Each time, the sound came from a different place... sometimes behind them, sometimes ahead, sometimes impossibly close, as if breathed directly into Tavian's ear.

Rovan cursed steadily under his breath, a litany of grounding profanity. "It's fishing," he muttered. "Trying to see what you'll bite on."

Tavian's hands shook. "It's not random."

"No," Rovan agreed. "It's precise."

They reached a bend in the road where the path dipped slightly before climbing again. Tavian slowed, eyes narrowing.

The ground ahead looked... wrong.

Not broken. Not altered.

Misremembered.

The stones seemed arranged differently than they had been moments before, as if the road had quietly reassembled itself while Tavian wasn't looking. A familiar curve now bent the opposite direction. A tree Tavian was certain had stood on the left now loomed on the right.

Rovan noticed his hesitation. "What?"

"The road," Tavian said. "It's trying to make me stop."

Rovan glanced around, scowling. "Looks like a road."

"That's the problem."

The voice returned, gentle now. Encouraging.

"You're almost there," it said. "Just rest a moment."

Rovan's hand closed hard around Tavian's forearm. "Eyes on me," he snapped. "Not the ground. Me."

Tavian obeyed.

Rovan's face was pale, drawn tight with effort, but it was *real*. The sight of it anchored Tavian more than he'd expected.

The pressure eased slightly.

They moved again.

The dark grew thicker as they climbed, not deepening so much as *gathering*. It felt less like absence and more like a substance; soft, compressible, aware of their passage.

Tavian's ribs pulsed once.

The cold brightness responded... not flaring, not pulling outward, but tightening, as if drawing itself inward around a core Tavian could not yet name.

Rovan noticed the change. "It's quieter."

"Yes," Tavian said. "Because it's closer."

The voice did not return.

That was worse.

They reached a stretch of road where the trees fell back slightly, revealing a long, shallow ravine cutting across the hillside. The ravine should have been empty.

It wasn't.

Darkness pooled there in a way Tavian had only seen once before, on a battlefield he'd tried very hard to forget. Not shadow. Not night.

A *concentration.*

The moonlight bent around it, skirting its edges as if unwilling to cross.

Rovan slowed to a stop. "That wasn't there before."

"No," Tavian said. "It's listening."

The dark in the ravine stirred, folding inward slightly, as if acknowledging the statement.

Tavian felt the pull intensify, not toward the ravine, but *through* him. Like a pressure differential suddenly equalizing.

He staggered.

Rovan grabbed him, hauling him back a step. "Stay with me!"

Tavian gasped, vision swimming. The cold brightness under his ribs surged, sharper now, responding to the proximity.

"It's not trying to take me," Tavian said through clenched teeth. "It's trying to... tune me."

Rovan swore. "Like an instrument."

"Yes."

The darkness in the ravine shifted again, forming a subtle spiral, edges drawing inward as if tracing a pattern Tavian could feel more than see.

The voice returned, not from the ravine, not from the trees, but from *everywhere* at once.

Faultlight.

The word landed like a weight dropped into still water.

Tavian's knees buckled.

Rovan dragged him backward, muscles straining. "Don't you dare answer that."

Tavian forced his breath steady, refusing to let the word echo back. He pictured it as the elder had framed it, not a name to be spoken, but a condition to be resisted.

The spiral in the ravine hesitated.

The voice pressed again, less confident now.

You are closer than you think.

Tavian laughed, short and breathless. "You don't know me as well as you think."

The pressure spiked.

Rovan's grip tightened to pain. "Tav…"

"I'm here," Tavian said, more to himself than to Rovan. He planted his boots, grounding himself against the pull. "I'm not open."

The dark recoiled slightly, as if testing a boundary it hadn't expected.

The spiral loosened.

The ravine dimmed.

For a moment, the road felt solid again.

Rovan sagged against Tavian, chest heaving. "That thing is *practicing*," he said. "It's not attacking. It's learning."

Tavian nodded, jaw tight. "Which means it's getting better."

They did not linger.

They moved past the ravine quickly, boots crunching on stone, neither looking back. The darkness did not follow, not immediately, but Tavian felt its attention remain, like a weight behind his eyes.

The watchtower rose ahead, stark against the night sky.

Its silhouette had changed.

Where once it had looked like a ruin, now it looked… *aligned*. The beams and stonework caught the moonlight in unnatural ways, edges sharpening, lines converging toward the platform at the top as if the structure itself were being drawn into purpose.

Rovan stared. "It's not just a tower anymore."

"No," Tavian said. "It's a focus."

The cold brightness beneath his ribs pulsed again, steady and insistent.

The voice did not return.

It didn't need to.

The watchtower waited.

And Tavian understood, with a clarity that made his stomach drop, that whatever choice he made up there would not just decide whether the night ended...

It would decide *how* the world learned to close its wounds.

They climbed the final rise in silence.

Behind them, the ravine lay still, its darkness loosening into something that resembled shadow again.

For now.

Chapter Eleven

The Long Vigil

They reached the tower long before the valley was ready to admit it had become the center of something.

The rise was steeper here, the steps cut into the hill worn smooth from old boots and older weather. The tower itself stood in silhouette against the thinning sky, stone ribs, timber bones, and the open platform above like a mouth waiting to speak.

Rovan stopped at the base, breathing hard.

Tavian didn't. Not because he wasn't tired, but because he had learned something in the last two days: fatigue was an honest sensation. Fear wasn't. Fear pretended to be exhaustion so it could make decisions for you.

He kept walking.

Rovan caught his sleeve. "Hold up."

Tavian paused, looking back.

Rovan's face was pale under the grime and dirt, the lines around his eyes deeper than they should've been. He had the look of a man trying to decide whether to run from a cliff or jump from it.

"You don't have to do it *now*," Rovan said. "We've still got…"

"No," Tavian replied, and the word came out calmer than he felt. "We don't."

Rovan's jaw tightened. "You sure?"

Tavian looked toward Blackmere.

The town sat below them like a cluster of dim lanterns and closed mouths. Smoke rose from chimneys in thin threads. No music. No laughter. No movement that wasn't careful.

They were waiting.

Not for salvation.

For an ending.

Tavian swallowed. "The valley's already leaning. You feel it?"

Rovan hesitated, then nodded once. "Feels like the air's got teeth."

Tavian almost smiled at that. Almost.

"It's not going to wait for dusk because we want it to," Tavian said. "It's already here. It's been here since the moment I stopped pretending it couldn't find me."

Rovan's hand fell away from Tavian's sleeve. He looked down at his own fingers as if surprised they were shaking.

"You know what's worse than it speaking?" Rovan asked.

Tavian didn't answer.

Rovan's eyes lifted. "It learning when we're quiet."

A cold pulse tightened beneath Tavian's ribs, small and involuntary. Not pain. Not glow. A shift in internal pressure, like something inside him had turned its head at the mention of silence.

Rovan saw the flicker of Tavian's reaction. His expression hardened. "There. That."

Tavian exhaled slowly. "It's listening."

"Yeah," Rovan said, voice rough. "And we're about to give it a front-row seat."

They stood at the base of the tower for a moment longer, neither climbing, neither retreating. The sky above them looked washed thin, pale and reluctant. The kind of light that didn't promise anything.

Tavian reached into his coat and touched the folded strip of cloth the elder had given him. The fabric was stiff, rough against his fingertips. The shallow cuts were still there, unchanged by time or touch.

A boundary, she'd called it.

Not protection. Not a charm.

A reminder.

Tavian's hand fell away from it.

Rovan watched him. "You gonna tell me what she said? The word?"

Tavian hesitated.

The elder had told him not to repeat it.

But the world had already repeated it, hadn't it? In that ravine. In that pressure behind his teeth. In the way the night gathered early like a storm that had learned hunger.

Tavian met Rovan's gaze. "It's faultlight."

Rovan's face changed, just a fraction. As if the word itself had weight.

"Sounds like a curse," Rovan said.

"It's worse," Tavian replied. "It's a condition."

Rovan swallowed. "And you're carrying it."

Tavian's mouth tightened. "Or it's carrying me."

They stood in silence again. The forest around them remained too still. No wind. No birds. Just the valley's breath held tight.

Then, faintly, Tavian heard it.

Not a voice.

A note.

Low, sustained, almost musical, like the beginning of a song played by a thing that did not understand music.

The tower answered it. A subtle vibration in the beams. A tension in the wood that made Tavian's bones ache.

Rovan went rigid. "That wasn't there a second ago."

Tavian nodded, throat tight. "It knows where we are."

Rovan cursed softly. "Of course it does."

The note deepened.

Tavian felt it press inside his skull like meaning without language. He wanted to close his eyes. He didn't. He forced himself to look at the tower's steps instead... something physical, something honest.

Rovan stepped closer, lowering his voice. "Before we go up, tell me something."

Tavian kept his gaze forward. "What?"

Rovan's words came out slow, deliberate. "All this time... you ever think I hated you?"

Tavian's chest tightened. Not with faultlight. With something older. Human.

"Yes," he admitted.

Rovan nodded once, as if confirming a calculation. "I did. For a long time."

Tavian flinched, but Rovan raised a hand.

"Listen," Rovan said. "I hated you because it was easier than hating what happened. Easier than hating that seam. Easier than admitting the world can break and not apologize."

Tavian swallowed, jaw tight.

Rovan's voice roughened. "But I followed you because I also knew something else."

"What?" Tavian asked.

Rovan's gaze locked onto him with a fierce, brutal honesty. "You were the only one of us who *heard it* and still tried to stop it. Everyone else either ran blind or froze. You..." Rovan shook his head. "You did what you always do. You tried to fix it."

Tavian's throat tightened. "And got everyone killed."

Rovan's expression sharpened. "No," he said. "They were dead the moment the sky tore. You just gave the rest of the world a chance not to follow them."

The words hit Tavian harder than anything the phenomenon had whispered.

He looked at Rovan and saw, for the first time in a long time, the man who'd fought beside him... scarred, broken, furious, but still capable of truth.

Rovan exhaled shakily. "I'm saying this now because if we go up there and it takes you, I don't want my last words to be hatred."

Tavian stared at him. He did not know what to say.

So he said the only thing that felt honest.

"Don't let it make you empty," Tavian whispered.

Rovan's mouth twisted. "Too late."

Tavian shook his head. "Not yet."

Rovan stared at him a long moment, then nodded once, like a soldier accepting orders he didn't like.

"All right," he said. "Then we climb."

They started up the steps.

The note deepened with each one, the vibration in the tower increasing until Tavian could feel it in his teeth. The air thinned. The sky above them looked scraped clean, as if the stars were being pushed away before they could appear.

Halfway up, Tavian's vision flickered.

Not blacking out... shifting.

For an instant, the wood beneath his boots looked like the rim of a crater. The railing above looked like broken spears. The sky looked folded.

Tavian grabbed the post, breathing hard.

Rovan's hand clamped onto his shoulder. "Tav."

Tavian swallowed. "I'm here."

Rovan leaned close. "You hear it again?"

Tavian nodded once.

Rovan's voice lowered to a rasp. "Then do what you did on that battlefield. Don't listen like it wants. Listen long enough to know where the edge is, then stop."

Tavian stared at him.

Rovan's eyes were bright with something Tavian hadn't expected to see there.

Faith.

Not in gods. Not in destiny.

In Tavian.

They climbed the last steps.

The platform waited above them like a verdict.

And as Tavian stepped onto it, the note in the air sharpened into an almost-audible harmony, and the valley's thin light withdrew another degree, as if night itself had been pulled closer by the throat.

Tavian stood on the boards and felt the world lean toward him.

Rovan stepped beside him, shoulder to shoulder.

"Ready?" Rovan whispered.

Tavian's mouth tasted faintly of iron, though he hadn't bitten his tongue.

"No," he said. "But I'm done running."

Below them, the forest's darkness shifted... slow, deliberate.

Something began to climb.

Chapter Twelve

The Watchtower

From the height of the tower, the forest pressed close on three sides, dark and dense, its edge uneven like a jawline.

And above it all, the sky had begun to do the wrong thing.

Stars should have appeared.

They didn't.

The heavens were not black... yet, but empty, a dull gray smear as if someone had wiped the night clean. The moon was absent. Not hidden. Absent.

Rovan stared upward, jaw clenched. "It's early."

Tavian's voice was thin. "It doesn't care about time."

Rovan looked at him sharply. "That's not an answer."

"It's the only one that fits."

The air tightened.

Not wind. Not cold.

A tightening, like the valley was being wrapped slowly in cloth. Tavian felt it press against his skin, not physically but perceptually, like a pressure that made thoughts heavier, harder to move.

He forced his mind into stillness. No bargaining. No internal prayers.

Just refusal.

A shape moved at the edge of the trees.

Tavian's pulse jumped.

Rovan's hand closed around his knife.

The shape did not step into view. It did not need to.

A shadow detached itself from the forest as if the darkness there had thickened and decided to travel. It glided across the scrub grass without sound, without disturbing a blade, approaching the hill with the slow certainty of something that had all the time in the world.

Tavian's breath caught.

The cold beneath his ribs pulsed in response... not bright, not outward, but present. An internal pressure answering an external one, like two magnets finding one another.

The shadow reached the base of the hill.

It stopped.

It did not look up. It did not raise a face.

It simply paused, as if listening.

Then the hum in the air deepened until it became a note... low, sustained, almost musical in its steadiness. The tower beams vibrated faintly beneath Tavian's boots.

Rovan steadied himself against the railing. "It's making the tower sing."

Tavian clenched his jaw. The note wasn't only in the wood. It was in his teeth. His ribs. The back of his eyes.

The darkness below lifted... not an arm, not a face, but a portion of itself rising like smoke drawn upward.

The note shifted, and the air between tower and shadow tightened into a thread.

Tavian felt it pull.

His stomach lurched as if gravity had changed direction.

He grabbed the railing, knuckles white, forcing his feet to remain planted. The wood creaked under his grip.

Rovan lunged, grabbing Tavian's other arm. "Hold!"

The pull intensified.

Tavian's chest burned... not heat, but strain, as if something inside him were being tugged toward the base of the hill. The cold pressure beneath his ribs sharpened. His vision pinched at the edges, tunneling toward the shadow.

Rovan's grip slipped slightly as Tavian's body lurched forward an inch.

"Tav!" Rovan shouted. "Fight it!"

Tavian tried.

The pressure in his skull increased, filling his thoughts with steady insistence.

Return. Return. Return.

Tavian's mouth opened before he could stop it. A word rose in his throat... an answer, an acknowledgement, a surrender.

He bit it off with his teeth.

Blood filled his mouth.

The taste grounded him.

He forced his mind into refusal. Not words. Not bargaining.

Just *no*.

The pull faltered, then surged again, stronger, as if impatience had replaced curiosity.

Below, the shadow shifted, expanding. The darkness around it thickened into a shape that almost resembled a body, tall and narrow, edges soft, as if it had not decided what form was necessary.

The world around it dimmed.

Grass bent toward it.

The sky above Tavian's head dulled further, gray deepening as if ink had been spilled into it.

Rovan's voice cracked. "It's pulling the night down."

Tavian gasped, blood still on his tongue.

The cold beneath his ribs pulsed in time with the note now, synchronized. Tavian felt himself being drawn into rhythm, like his body was being tuned to match.

He understood with sick clarity that the phenomenon was not dragging him with brute force.

It was aligning him.

Making him fit.

Tavian's vision flickered. For a blink, the platform was the battlefield. For a blink, the railing was the rim of a crater. For a blink, he could smell smoke and iron and hear men screaming behind him.

He felt, horrifyingly, the old curiosity trying to return.

Rovan slapped Tavian's cheek hard.

The crack jolted Tavian back into pain, into the platform, into the present.

"What the hell are you doing?" Rovan hissed. "Stay with me!"

Tavian blinked, stunned.

Rovan's eyes were wet. "Don't you leave me here with that thing."

The plea hit Tavian harder than the slap.

He swallowed blood and forced his breath steady.

"No," Tavian rasped. "I'm here."

Rovan shifted his stance, bracing his boots against the boards, using his whole body as an anchor. His shoulder pressed into Tavian's side, and Tavian felt the tremor running through him... fear, exhaustion, something like determination.

Rovan was paying for every second he stayed.

The cold brightness in Tavian's chest surged again. This time it bled faintly through cloth, a pale, internal glow, as if the skin over his sternum had become thin.

Rovan saw it and went pale. "Gods."

The shadow at the base of the hill lifted again, and the air tightened into a thread so taut Tavian felt it in his jaw.

The voice arrived in Tavian's skull... not a sound, but understanding.

Return what broke.

Tavian's eyes snapped open.

Rovan stared at him. "You heard it."

Tavian nodded once, unable to speak.

The voice sharpened... closer now, less patient.

Close what you opened.

Tavian's stomach twisted. He understood what it meant. Mechanically. Not metaphor.

It wanted him to complete a motion he had interrupted long ago. To finish a crossing. To shut a door that had been left halfway.

And if he did...

Blackmere would be the first thing swallowed.

Tavian's gaze flicked to the dim coals of town below. He thought of the boy's unblinking eyes. Of doors gouged and splintered. Of Halde's stubborn refusal to be soft. Of the elder's hard choices.

He thought of Rovan Hollow... still holding him, refusing to let go.

The pull surged again, violent now, and Tavian felt Rovan's grip start to fail.

Rovan grunted, teeth bared, fighting to stay upright. "Tavian... do something!"

Tavian's breath came ragged. The elder's warning returned like a lifeline.

It cannot take what you do not offer.

He released the railing.

Rovan swore, panic flashing. "Tav!"

Tavian stepped forward.

Not toward the stairs. Toward the edge of the platform, directly above the hill.

The pull strengthened instantly, eager.

Tavian leaned into it as if walking into heavy wind.

Rovan grabbed him harder, nearly yanking him backward. "Don't!"

Tavian turned his head just enough to meet Rovan's gaze.

"I'm not giving it what it wants," Tavian said.

Rovan's face twisted. "Then what are you doing?"

Tavian swallowed, throat tight. "I'm making it come to me."

Rovan stared, horror and understanding colliding. "You're drawing it up here."

"Yes," Tavian said. "Where it can't test doors. Where it can't wear voices. Where it has to face me clean."

Rovan's grip trembled. "And what if it takes you clean?"

Tavian's lips pulled into something like a smile, bitter and exhausted. "Then at least it stops pretending it's not."

The sky above them deepened another shade.

The note sharpened.

The darkness at the base of the hill began to climb... night sliding uphill as if gravity had reversed, the grass bowing beneath it, the world tightening around its ascent.

Rovan leaned close, voice shaking. "If you hear it speak, don't answer."

Tavian swallowed blood, nodded once.

And as the darkness reached the first step of the tower, Tavian Calder stood at the edge of the platform and waited for the light to break.

Chapter Thirteen

Of Blood and Broken Light

✝

The darkness climbed like a thing with purpose.

It did not rush. It did not lunge. It did not behave like hunger.

It behaved like *return*.

The first step of the tower went black… not shadow, not absence of light, but a presence that made the wood's grain disappear. The second step followed. Then the third.

Tavian felt each one as a tightening in his ribs.

Rovan's grip bruised his arm. "It's climbing," he said, as if naming it could make it stop.

The note in the air rose, and the tower answered it with a faint vibration that ran through Tavian's boots and up his bones. The rails trembled. The nails in the boards seemed to hum.

Tavian's mouth was still full of blood where he'd bitten his own tongue earlier. The metallic taste anchored him. Kept him from drifting into the same blank curiosity the phenomenon seemed to invite.

He kept his eyes open.

He kept his mind closed.

The darkness reached the platform.

For a heartbeat, nothing happened.

It just... arrived.

The air thickened. The last of the day's color washed away, leaving the world in gray relief. Not night, not fully, but a thinning so complete it felt like the valley had been drained of its future.

The shape rose from the stairs without stepping, gathering itself into a tall, narrow form that suggested a body without committing to one. Edges softened and sharpened with each breath Tavian took, as though it was learning him by watching.

Rovan's breath stuttered. "Tav..."

The shape paused at the platform's edge.

It did not have eyes.

Tavian still knew it was looking at him.

The pressure in his skull returned, heavier than before... not pain, not force, but meaning pressing against the inside of his thoughts.

And with it, the voice.

Not spoken.

Understood.

Close what you broke.

Tavian's jaw clenched.

He remembered the elder's words... *answer with refusal, with certainty, with will,* and tried to gather himself into a single hard line.

No.

The note in the air changed, becoming softer, almost patient.

Return what is missing.

Rovan made a strangled sound. "It's talking to you."

Tavian didn't look away from the shape. "It's trying to."

Rovan's grip tightened, as if holding Tavian could anchor him to being human. "Don't listen."

Tavian swallowed blood. "I'm not."

The shape leaned forward slightly.

The world leaned with it.

The railings creaked, wood protesting as if a pressure had been applied from every direction. The darkness did not push with strength. It pushed with alignment, making the air behave differently, making gravity choose a new preference.

Tavian's chest flared cold. The glow beneath his skin sharpened, a pale line beneath his sternum.

Rovan saw it and went pale. "It's brighter."

Tavian didn't answer.

Inside him, something stirred... not like a parasite, not like a tumor. Like a memory in the wrong place.

The voice returned, quieter now, intimate in a way that felt obscene.

You are open. You are the hinge. Let the seam mend.

Tavian's vision flickered.

For a blink, the platform was the battlefield.

For a blink, the tower rails were the broken rim of a crater.

For a blink, the air smelled of smoke and iron and the sharp sweetness of blood.

He saw the seam in the sky again... folded, luminous, unbearable.

He saw himself step forward.

Listening.

And he saw the moment he had never fully remembered, the moment of rupture inside him.

Not the sky breaking.

Him breaking.

A sensation like overstretched fabric ripping.

A sudden, violent lightness in his chest as something was pulled out of him.

Not taken.

Separated.

Tavian's breath hitched.

Rovan's voice cut through. "Tav... where are you?"

Tavian blinked hard, forcing the battlefield away. The tower returned, trembling. The shape in the darkness held still, waiting as if it knew Tavian had just reached the correct door inside his own mind.

"You remember," Rovan whispered.

Tavian didn't answer with words.

He shook.

Not with fear, with recognition.

The cold brightness in his ribs wasn't foreign.

It wasn't a mark.

It wasn't a curse.

It was a piece of him that had been ripped loose the night the seam opened... something that should have remained inside him, bound to his breath and blood and bone.

His missing weight.

His missing balance.

No wonder the phenomenon followed.

It wasn't tracking prey.

It was tracking *incompletion*.

Tavian's throat tightened. He spoke aloud, voice ragged. "It's not yours."

The shape stilled.

Rovan stared. "What?"

Tavian kept his eyes on the darkness. "It thinks it's returning something," he said. "But it doesn't understand what it's returning."

The note in the air sharpened.

Return. Mend.

Tavian felt the pull intensify, tugging at his chest as if the cold brightness beneath his skin wanted to leap forward and join the darkness.

Not because it belonged to the darkness.

Because it belonged to *wholeness*.

Rovan stepped closer, his hand finding Tavian's shoulder again, grounding him with pressure. "You don't have to give it anything."

Tavian swallowed. "That's the problem."

Rovan's eyes narrowed. "What problem?"

Tavian's voice came out low. "It isn't asking."

The darkness moved.

Not stepping, shifting. Folding toward Tavian as if the space between them could be reduced by will alone.

The rails groaned. The tower shuddered.

Rovan drew his knife, though the gesture felt like a prayer more than a plan. "Back," he snarled at the shape, as if it could hear sound.

The shape did not react to steel.

It reacted to Tavian.

It leaned closer. The air tightened, compressing breath in Tavian's lungs. The note in the world rose higher, approaching something like a scream held carefully inside glass.

Tavian's chest brightened. The pale line beneath his skin flared, cold, sharp, bright enough now that it made the wood around him cast thin shadows.

Rovan swore, voice cracking. "Tavian!"

Tavian forced himself to breathe through it.

He understood now what the elder meant: *It cannot take what you do not offer.*

But refusal was not simply saying no.

Refusal was owning what was inside him.

Claiming it.

Naming it as his.

Tavian closed his eyes.

Not to flee.

To focus.

He pictured the cold brightness under his ribs... not as a curse, not as a foreign thing, but as a piece of himself that had been torn away. He imagined it stitched back into him, not by surrendering to the darkness, but by pulling it inward through sheer will.

His breath steadied.

The pressure in his skull bucked, confused.

The voice inside him sharpened. *Return.*

Tavian opened his eyes.

"No," he said clearly.

The word landed like a hammer.

The note in the air faltered.

The darkness paused, as if surprised.

Rovan stared at Tavian like he'd never seen him before.

Tavian kept his gaze on the shape. "You can't mend me," he said, voice gaining strength. "You can't complete what you don't understand."

The cold brightness surged again, trying to rise.

Tavian clenched his jaw and pulled it back inward... *not physically*, but with the deep instinct of a man refusing to be moved.

Blood ran from where he'd bitten his tongue, warm now against the cold in his chest.

The light beneath his skin flickered, then steadied, no longer pulling outward.

Holding.

The darkness shifted, and for the first time Tavian felt something like resistance in it... not anger, not hunger, but disorientation.

A phenomenon meeting a boundary it hadn't expected.

Rovan's voice was hoarse. "What are you doing?"

Tavian didn't look away. "Taking myself back."

The words tasted strange and right.

The world tightened again, but differently, like a rope being pulled and finding it cannot shorten any further.

The shape leaned in closer.

Tavian felt the air compress.

And then, suddenly, it was *there*.

Not at the platform's edge.

At Tavian's chest.

The darkness touched him without hands.

Cold pressed through cloth and skin and bone, seeking the pale line beneath.

Tavian's vision flashed white... not bright, but empty, like paper.

He felt the cold brightness inside him strain, trying to detach.

Rovan shouted, lunging, grabbing Tavian around the waist from behind, anchoring him with his whole weight.

"Hold!" Rovan screamed. "Hold!"

Tavian ground his teeth, blood and breath and will blending into a single hard refusal.

He pictured the cold brightness as a wound he had carried too long without acknowledging. He pictured closing his fingers around it inside his own ribs... not to crush it, not to destroy it, but to *claim* it.

Mine.

The thought hit like thunder.

The cold brightness flared, then folded inward suddenly, drawing tight against Tavian's heart as if finding its place.

The pale line under his skin dimmed sharply.

The darkness recoiled.

Not dramatically... subtly, like a hand pulling back from a hot stove.

The note in the air snapped into silence.

The tower stopped vibrating.

For a heartbeat, the world held perfectly still.

Then the sky above the valley shuddered, just a ripple, like cloth settling after strain.

Stars appeared.

Faint at first, then clearer. Cold pinpricks in a newly honest night.

Rovan's grip loosened. He sagged behind Tavian, breath ragged, as if he'd been holding the whole world up.

Tavian stared at the shape.

It had changed.

It did not feel smaller, but it felt less certain; its edges less committed, its presence no longer pressing forward.

The voice returned one last time, not as command but as question.

Incomplete...?

Tavian swallowed, throat raw. "Not anymore."

The darkness lingered, as if listening for an opening.

Tavian gave it none.

Slowly, like a tide receding, the shape withdrew... not down the stairs, not into the forest, but into itself. The blackness compressed, folding into a narrower column until it was nothing more than a stain at the base of the tower steps.

Then even that faded, leaving only ordinary night.

Rovan slid to sit on the platform boards, head bowed, shaking. "What... what did you do?"

Tavian's chest ached... not cold now, but sore, like a muscle finally used after years of atrophy.

"I stopped treating it like something separate," Tavian said quietly.

Rovan lifted his head, eyes bloodshot. "You took it back."

Tavian stared out over Blackmere.

The town below looked unchanged, but the valley's silence felt different, less tight, less watchful. The lamps in the distance burned straighter now, their flames no longer leaning toward the forest.

Tavian exhaled slowly.

"I think," he said, and his voice surprised him with its steadiness, "it was never trying to punish me."

Rovan barked a laugh that held no humor. "Comforting."

Tavian glanced at him. "No." He looked back toward the dark treeline. "Just true."

Rovan's hand trembled as he wiped his mouth. "So what now?"

Tavian listened to his own breath.

No hum.

No pressure behind his eye.

No cold awareness under his ribs.

Only the ordinary weight of being alive.

"We go back," Tavian said.

Rovan stared. "You think they'll let you?"

Tavian's gaze hardened. "They'll have to."

Below, the first rooster crowed, too early, confused by the sudden return of natural rhythm.

Tavian stood.

His legs were unsteady, but he was not being pulled anymore.

He looked once more into the forest.

The darkness stared back, but it did not lean.

And in that quiet, Tavian Calder understood the cruelest truth of all:

What had followed him was not hatred.

It was the world trying to close a wound, without caring what it would cut away in the process.

Chapter Fourteen

Unbroken

They returned to Blackmere under a sky that remembered how to be night.

Stars hung cold and steady above the valley, sharp points of light that did not bend or smear. The moon, thin as a knife edge, rode low over the treeline. It looked indifferent, which was the first mercy Tavian had felt in days.

Rovan walked beside him without speaking. His hands still shook. Not from drink, not tonight, but from the aftermath of holding onto a man while the world tried to pull him apart.

Tavian felt the absence inside his chest like a bruise. Not emptiness, wholeness. A weight that had returned to where it belonged, sore from being missing too long.

They reached the first houses before dawn.

Doors were still barred, but the air no longer held that tight, listening pressure. The lamps visible through cracks in shutters burned upright. Their flames did not lean toward anything unseen.

Rovan noticed it too. He exhaled, shoulders loosening just slightly. "They'll feel it," he said.

"They'll doubt it," Tavian replied. "Fear doesn't let go quickly."

Rovan gave a humorless huff. "Neither do people."

The square was half-lit by lanterns. A few figures moved carefully, as if afraid that stepping too hard would break whatever fragile calm had returned. The elder stood by the well, staff planted, wrapped in her shawl. Mistress Halde leaned in the doorway of The Latch, arms folded, face carved out of stubbornness.

When Tavian stepped into the square, heads turned.

A murmur rippled.

He saw the same fear he'd left behind. But beneath it, something else.

Confusion.

Because the valley felt different, and they could not explain it.

A man shoved forward from the edge of the crowd, eyes wild, rope in his hand. "He's back," the man hissed. "After all that, he's back."

The rope twitched like a living thing.

Tavian didn't flinch.

Rovan shifted, ready to intercept. Tavian raised one hand slightly, stopping him without looking.

The elder's voice cut through. "Put that down."

The man hesitated. "Elder..."

"Put. It. Down."

The rope fell from his hand as if it had burned him.

Halde's gaze stayed on Tavian, hard and searching. "Did it take you?" she asked.

Tavian met her eyes. "No."

"And the night?" Halde demanded. "Is it gone?"

Tavian listened.

No hum.

No pull.

No leaning lamps.

He looked up at the sky. The stars held steady.

"Yes," he said. "It's gone."

The crowd murmured, disbelief fighting with relief. Someone laughed once high and trembling. Someone else began to cry quietly, the sound muffled like shame.

A woman pushed through the circle, clutching her shawl tight around her shoulders. "My door," she said, voice shaking. "The gouges..."

She pointed toward the road her house was on.

Tavian nodded once. "Check them."

A man took two cautious steps backward, then turned and ran toward the lane. Another followed. Then another. A strange urgency moved through them, the need to confirm that the world had stopped pressing.

The elder did not move. Her eyes stayed on Tavian.

"You did something," she said quietly.

Tavian exhaled. "I stopped giving it room."

Her gaze sharpened, as if she understood more than she wanted to admit. "And the thing in you?"

Tavian's hand drifted to his sternum, pressing lightly.

Nothing answered.

"It's mine," he said. "And it's quiet now."

Rovan let out a shaky breath beside him, as if he'd been holding it since the tower.

The elder nodded, once. Not approval. Recognition.

Halde stepped away from the doorway then, approaching Tavian until they stood within arm's reach. Her torchlight threw sharp lines across her face, making her look carved from oak.

"You're leaving," she said.

It wasn't a question.

Tavian nodded. "If I stay, fear will keep trying to make sense of me."

Halde's jaw tightened. "That's not an answer."

"It's the only one that fits," Tavian said, and surprised himself with a faint echo of humor.

Halde looked him over once more, the posture, the stillness, the eyes that no longer flinched when the lamps hissed. Something in her expression shifted, just enough to suggest reluctant respect.

"Then go," she said. "But don't ever bring your trouble back here."

Tavian met her gaze. "I won't."

Halde's eyes narrowed. "You promise?"

Tavian held her eyes steadily. "I promise."

The elder lifted her staff slightly, drawing Tavian's attention. "One more thing."

Tavian turned to her.

She held out the older strip of cloth, the one she'd given him, stiff and marked with those shallow cuts. Tavian reached for it.

The elder did not let go.

"You will keep it," she said. "Not because it protects you."

Tavian waited.

"Because it reminds you," she continued, "that there are things in this world older than your guilt. And they do not care how righteous you are." Her voice softened, a rare thing. "Only how open."

Tavian nodded slowly. "I understand."

The elder released the cloth.

Rovan shifted, clearing his throat. "What about him?" he asked, nodding toward the tavern.

Halde's eyes flicked to Rovan. "What about him?"

Rovan rubbed a trembling hand over his jaw. "He can't... keep living like this."

Halde snorted. "He has been."

Rovan's mouth tightened. "Not well."

Halde studied him for a long moment, then jerked her chin toward the tavern. "If you want stew, come earn it. If you want to keep drinking yourself blind, do it somewhere else. I'm not hosting your slow suicide anymore."

Rovan stared at her, shocked. Then his shoulders sagged and he let out a sound that might have been a laugh, might have been something else.

"Fair," he rasped.

Halde's gaze returned to Tavian. "And you," she said. "You'll be the kind of man who doesn't come back."

Tavian swallowed. The truth of it sat heavy.

"Yes," he said.

Halde nodded once, then turned away.

The crowd had thinned. People drifted toward their homes, toward their doors, toward the marks carved into their thresholds, touching them with shaking fingers as if to confirm they were still there.

Tavian watched them for a moment, then turned toward the eastern road.

Rovan fell into step beside him.

"You don't have to," Tavian said.

Rovan snorted. "Don't start with me."

Tavian glanced over. "You're staying."

"I am," Rovan replied. He hesitated, then added, "At least for now."

Tavian nodded. "Then don't waste it."

Rovan's mouth tightened. "Don't tell me how to live."

Tavian gave the faintest smile. "Then live."

They walked to the edge of town together, the first pale hint of dawn beginning to press against the horizon.

At the fork in the road, Rovan stopped.

Tavian did too.

Rovan stared at him for a long moment, eyes bloodshot, jaw clenched as if he had to force the words out.

"You didn't run," Rovan said.

Tavian's throat tightened. "I did."

Rovan shook his head. "You stopped."

Tavian exhaled slowly. "Only because you held on."

Rovan looked away, swallowing hard. "Someone had to."

They stood in silence as the dawn grew stronger, light returning in honest layers.

Tavian tucked the marked cloth into his coat.

Rovan lifted a hand, then dropped it. "Where will you go?"

Tavian looked east, toward roads he did not know, toward towns that had never heard the name Blackmere, toward skies that might one day fold the wrong way again.

"Anywhere the light breaks clean," he said.

Rovan nodded once, as if the answer was both promise and warning.

Tavian turned and began walking.

After a few steps, he glanced back.

Rovan Hollow stood at the fork, a dark shape against the growing dawn. For a moment he looked like he might call out, might reach for something to anchor him.

Instead he simply raised two fingers in a gesture that was not quite a salute, not quite a farewell.

Tavian returned it and kept walking.

The sun crested the ridge, and the valley brightened.

This time the light did not retreat.

And for the first time since the sky split and something bright and wrong crawled through, Tavian Calder stepped into dawn without flinching... unbroken.

Chapter Fifteen

Epilogue

Blackmere learned how to sleep again.

Not quickly. Not easily. But in pieces.

The first night after the tower, no one lit lamps at all. Doors stayed barred long past dawn. People sat in the dark with their backs to walls, listening for a hum that did not come. Some swore they could still feel the air leaning, as if the valley itself had not yet decided whether to relax.

By the third night, someone lit a single lamp.

It burned straight.

That was when the rumors began to shift.

They spoke of the tower first, how the wood no longer vibrated, how the stone felt ordinary again beneath the hand. They spoke of the forest, quieter now, shadows falling where they were meant to fall. They spoke of the ravine along the western road, which had collapsed into nothing more than dirt and rock, as if the darkness there had never gathered at all.

They did not speak Tavian Calder's name.

Some said he had been taken. Others said he had been given back. A few insisted he had never been real in the first place, only a story the town had told itself when fear needed a face.

The elder corrected none of them.

She walked the lanes each morning with her staff tapping stone, checking doors.

The gouges were still there.

Deep lines in wood, torn and measured, scars that had not softened with time. Some tried to sand them down. The grain resisted. Others nailed planks over them, pretending the marks were rot or accident.

The elder let them try.

On the seventh day, a child asked her why the marks remained if the night was gone.

The elder looked at the door a long moment before answering.

"Because memory doesn't leave when danger does," she said. "It stays to teach the hands."

The child nodded as if this made sense.

Mistress Halde reopened The Latch a week later.

The first night back, she lit every lamp at once and watched them carefully, daring the flames to lean. When they did not, she poured herself a drink and did not dilute it.

Rovan Hollow came to the door at dusk.

He looked different. Not healed, nothing so neat, but steadier, like a man whose weight had redistributed itself after years of leaning the wrong way. He did not ask for drink. He asked for stew.

Halde studied him, then set a bowl in front of him without comment.

Rovan ate slowly, as if relearning the shape of hunger.

"You staying?" she asked.

"For now," he said.

Halde grunted. "Don't make a habit of almost dying for other people."

Rovan gave a thin smile. "I'll try something new."

At the edge of town, the eastern road lay open again.

Grass had begun to reclaim its ruts. Stones sat where they always had. The path did not twist or misremember itself. Travelers passed through once more, careful at first, then with increasing confidence.

Some asked about the gouges on doors.

The townsfolk told them it was an old custom.

No one explained further.

On a quiet morning, the elder stood alone before Tavian Calder's door.

The marks there were deeper than the rest.

She traced them with her fingers... not testing, not erasing. Remembering.

Then she took a small knife from her shawl and added a fourth cut.

Careful. Deliberate.

When she was done, she pressed her palm flat against the wood and closed her eyes.

"Counted," she murmured.

The valley did not answer.

Far from Blackmere, Tavian walked beneath a sky that had not folded yet.

He followed no road for long. When paths branched, he chose the one that felt less certain. He slept where he could and moved on when he needed to. He listened more than he spoke.

Sometimes, at night, he felt the old pressure, faint now, like a scar tightening with weather.

He did not fight it.

He acknowledged it.

He had learned the difference.

In one town, he saw doors marked with shallow lines that looked almost familiar. In another, he heard a story about a night when the stars vanished and the lamps bowed as if in prayer. In a third, a woman told him of a brightness that had come through a church roof and left the stone warm for years afterward.

Tavian listened.

He did not name what he heard.

He did not need to.

One evening, as he passed a roadside house at dusk, he noticed something that made him stop.

A single door bore marks that were not weathered.

They were new.

Three vertical cuts, crossed once.

Tavian stood there for a long time, watching the light retreat from the fields. He felt no pull. No hum. No pressure behind his eyes.

Only the quiet knowledge that the world did not break in only one place.

He turned away before night fell.

Behind him, the door remained closed.

And somewhere, not near Blackmere, not near the tower, but close enough to matter, the dark leaned, listening.

Not to him.

Not yet.

Afterword

There are accounts that end with answers, and there are accounts that end with endurance. This is the latter.

What has been preserved here does not resolve cleanly because the events themselves did not. Those who passed through them did not leave unchanged, and neither did the places that bore witness. Some choices were made in urgency. Others were made in fear, or in hope, or in the quiet belief that there would be time to correct them later. In many cases, there was not.

It is tempting to search these fragments for a single turning point... a moment when everything might have gone differently. Such moments rarely announce themselves. More often, consequence accumulates slowly, layered decision upon decision, until the weight becomes visible only in hindsight.

What remains is not a lesson, but a record.

Light, once broken, does not simply return to its former shape. It lingers where it fractured, altering what passes through it afterward. The same may be said of those who stood too close, and of the world that continued on around them.

This account ends here because the surviving material does. Beyond this point, the record thins. What follows belongs to other witnesses, other fractures, and other reckonings, some preserved, many not.

If there is a comfort to be found, it lies in this: endurance itself leaves a trace.

A Note on Risenfell

The account presented here concerns only a narrow fracture within a much broader record.

Risenfell is not a single place, nor a single moment, but a convergence of realms shaped by forces that resist stable naming. Boundaries shift. Measures of time fail to align. What one record describes as distance, another preserves as duration. These inconsistencies are not errors, but reflections of the conditions under which the accounts were formed.

Across surviving material, certain patterns recur. Light appears not merely as illumination, but as structure... binding, dividing, and, at times, failing. Where it thins, histories diverge. Where it breaks, consequence takes root.

Some realms preserved order through erasure. Others through record, delay, or imposed stability. Each believed their method sufficient. None were untouched by what followed.

This volume does not attempt to catalogue these realms, nor to reconcile their contradictions. It stands instead as one preserved instance among many... one account of what occurs when fracture is mistaken for control, and endurance for resolution.

Further materials remain.

They are incomplete.

They are inconsistent.

They are waiting.

Additional materials related to this volume and the broader Risenfell record may be accessed through the publisher's archive at **risenfell.com**

About the Curator

Aldric Thorn is not the author of the account presented here.

The role of curator is one of selection, preservation, and restraint. The materials attributed to Risenfell were gathered across years from private collections, damaged archives, oral transmission, and sources whose original context has not survived. In many cases, attribution was incomplete or deliberately absent.

No attempt has been made to standardize these materials beyond what was necessary for readability. Variations in language, sequence, and emphasis remain where they insist upon remaining. Where certainty could not be established, it was not supplied.

The curator's work is ongoing.

Additional fragments continue to surface... some corroborating, others in open contradiction. Whether these represent parallel accounts, regional divergence, or deeper structural fracture remains unresolved.

Readers should understand that absence is not an oversight. It is part of the record.

www.ingramcontent.com/pod-product-compliance
Lightning Source LLC
Chambersburg PA
CBHW020045310726

48970CB00007B/2421